cranachan

For Mrs Stewart,
who first introduced me to the poetry of Robert Burns
during a memorable year in Primary Four.

"Hey, Rab, d'you think if we dig deep enough we'll find buried treasure?"

Gil poked the hard mud again with his hoe, upsetting the piles of stones Rab was trying to rake into his basket. Rab rolled his eyes at his younger brother and set to work picking them up one by one.

"We can dig all the way from Scotland to India and we still willnae find the brains you're missing, you wee daftie," he muttered.

Clearing rocks from the barren field was back-breaking work, and Rab was ready to drop from exhaustion. He was starting to regret picking up all the biggest stones to save his brother's smaller arms. Gil still had plenty of air left in his lungs to blether, and Rab was too tired to keep up with his endless chatter.

"But back in the days of adventure, when William Wallace and his brave lads were running about the country fighting the invaders, maybe they hid some of their stash in the countryside, for safe keeping, y'know?" Gil said eagerly, too excited by the thought of ancient gold to notice Rab was ready to clobber him for prattling instead of working.

"Aye, that's right. Maybe the bravest hero in all of Scotland chose this God-forsaken spit of farmland to bury his army's money hundreds of years afore," Rab snorted. "Maybe it's no a worthless piece of dirt in the middle of nowhere after all. Maybe it's a treasure chest waiting to be opened. So go find it, Gil. Get digging." Rab gave his brother a shove, directing him to the next patch to be cleared.

"Ach, Rab, you're no fun anymore," Gil grumbled. "It's no that bad here, is it?"

Rab's only reply was to toss another stone into his basket so hard that it bounced out again. He sighed wearily and stretched, trying to iron out all the kinks that had turned his back into a scrunched-up accordion. Gil already knew the answer to that question anyhow. They both missed their old life in the cottage at Alloway, with the school across the road and their friends living nearby, ready for a game of soldiers after lessons. Here, life was a fight for survival like nothing Rab had ever known.

Mount Oliphant looked pretty enough in October, Rab could admit that at least. The sun shone gold on the newly harvested fields, and a flock of wild geese looked like tiny sailboats swimming across the endless blue of the sky. It seemed like the heavens were smiling down on the farm they'd moved to. But Rab knew the prettiness was all just a trick of the light, hiding the rotten truth beneath.

The land was so poor it was sucking the life from them and their father as they toiled over it, and in the winter their hilltop farm did little to keep the cold and damp from the family huddled inside. Even the princely sum of the hundred pounds their father had borrowed from their landlord hadn't been enough to keep up with repairs, and now they had heavy debt to add to their struggles.

"It's a rare sight, though, is it no?" Gill tried again, nudging Rab and trying to coax a smile from him.

"Aye, it's no bad," Rab had to admit.

The one thing their farm had going for it was the view. Looking west in the full glow of autumn was enough to lift Rab's spirits no matter how tired he was. The Atlantic Ocean stretched out to the distant horizon, the sea wind whispering stories of daring and adventure in the boys' ears as they worked. South-west towards the Heads of Ayr, small farms nestled in the gently rolling hills, and flocks of birds sought shelter there from the storms that rolled in from the coast.

Nothing excited Rab more than the sight of the bustling town of Ayr in the distance. He couldn't see the busy streets and markets, or the old bridge across the river that had been patched so many times it was a wonder it hadn't crumbled beneath the cart wheels crossing it. But he knew exactly where the town lay, as it was marked out by the tollbooth spire, and the old baronial tower they'd nicknamed the 'Wallace Tower'.

Whenever he looked at it, Rab was reminded of his hero's adventures, and his pulse would quicken in excitement as he remembered the stories of daring and danger he'd read.

"You know whit Wallace would tell you if he was passing through here with his army nowadays?" Rab said.

"Whit?" Gil asked.

"He'd say you were a lazy wee gowk with no more sense than a turnip."

"And he'd say you were a big lump with straw for brains," Gil grinned back.

"Did you just declare war on me, you wee bogle?"

"Aye, I did. Whit'll you do about it?"

"Knock your head in!" Rab laughed, aiming a playful blow that Gil sidestepped easily.

"Prepare to do or die!" Gil yelled, launching himself at Rab with his hoe held like a sword. The clattering of wood scared the crows from the field as the boys danced through the mud. They were no longer two labourers with farm tools, but brave soldiers fighting for their lives with flashing steel.

"I'm William Wallace, and this land is mine!" Gil roared.

"No! I'm twelve and more, so I'm William Wallace, and you're the invader!" Rab fired back.

"No fear! I'm turned eleven, so I'm—Aw, jings!" Gil cried when he swung his hoe too hard at Rab's rake and snapped it in half.

"Now you've gone and done it," Rab groaned. "Wait till Pa sees this! He'll—"

"BOYS! Whit in the name of goodness are you up to?"

Rab and Gil had been too busy re-enacting the battle of Stirling Bridge to notice the sound of horses' hooves approaching. They turned to see their father in the lane, leading the plough horses to the far fields. Rab's cheeks went red with shame, but Gil was too young to notice the tired lines etched into their father's face, and the sweat that dripped from his brow from the wheat threshing he'd been hard at all morning.

"It wasnae me," Gil cried, "it was Rab! He started it."

"And I'm ending it!" William Burns growled. "You're no wee bairns; you're old enough to be trusted in the fields without me keeping an eye on you. Lord knows I've got enough to do myself as it is."

He was speaking to both of them, but Rab knew the rebuke was aimed at him as the eldest. He dropped his eyes to the ground, mumbling, "Sorry, Pa. I'll take the hoe to the smithy to get patched tomorrow."

"Aye, and how much'll that cost? We can ill afford waste, Rab."

Rab swallowed hard, guilt turning his tongue to heavy lead.

"Come with me, Gilbert. The far fields need ploughed, and you've still a deal to learn about keeping the furrow straight. Get back to work, Rab. That field needs cleared by the end of the week so I can lime it afore I sow the winter crop."

Gil was only too happy to hand Rab his broken hoe and follow his father down the lane. Rab watched them disappear behind the hedgerows, the guilt and shame leaving a bitter taste in his mouth. Life here was all work, and even five minutes of fun was too much to ask. And as for school and any real learning? He could forget about that.

I may no have straw for brains yet, but if I keep at this mindless work much longer then all the knowledge'll be threshed out of my head, and bare stalks of learning will be all that's left, Rab thought, kicking hard at a stone in his way and stubbing his toe through his worn boot. *It's no fair! Other fathers can afford to hire labourers, and their boys can go to school. If we hadnae moved to this midden of a farm then—*

"Hey, Rab!" a girl's voice called. "Are you ready to take a wee break?"

"Clear off, Agnes, I'm busy," Rab snapped, aiming his anger at his younger sister who came trotting into the field in a pair of clogs that belonged to their mother.

"I know you are, you big bletherskate. That's why I'm bringing you a basket. Will you no take a wee bite? Ma's too busy with the baby and the bairns to fix a midday meal at the house for you all."

"Leave it down then," Rab muttered, "and I'll maybe have it later." His stomach was rumbling loudly, and the oat scone and corked bottle of broth looked tasty. But he was still too sore from his father's telling off to have any kind words for his sister.

"You're an ungrateful toad, Rab Burns!" Agnes dumped the scone and soup bottle down on a rock and clomped away across the mud.

"And you're a sharp-tongued wee shrew!" Rab called back. "Stop gadding about the fields and go and help Ma in the house with the wee ones like you're supposed to."

Agnes turned back and stuck her tongue out at him, then ran off down the lane. The sound of the wooden shoes tripping across the stones disappeared into the distance, and Rab's anger faded along with it. She was gone before Rab could call her back and tell her he didn't mean it, and thank her for thinking of him when she had so much else to do at home.

Bad soil and poverty dinnae just make for poor crops, he thought as he sat down on the rock and ate his lunch. *It's making me grow crooked too. I've been crabbit with the wee ones all summer, since afore the harvest.*

The baby coming in June hadn't helped. He knew

a new life was a blessing, but he had five brothers and sisters already, and Isabella crying through the night when they were all exhausted hadn't helped anyone's mood.

Late evening, when the younger children were in bed, was the only time he had to himself for his precious reading, and he'd been too tired to focus on books for months.

Maybe things'll get better when Isabella's a bit older and Ma and Pa aren't so tired, he thought.

Maybe if I help Pa with the threshing this year he'll have more time to help with my studies and I'll no wish for school so much.

Maybe if I give Agnes some of my tatties at dinner she'll no still be cross with me.

Maybe...

The only certain thing was that Rab had a whole field of stones to clear by the end of the week and sitting around daydreaming wasn't going to shift any rocks.

He picked up his rake and set to work again, determined to ignore the ache in his back and the sting in his hands each time the metal head hit a buried rock and sent a jolt of pain up his arms.

By the time the sun was setting, and his father and Gil had returned with the horses, Rab had cleared half the field, and was rewarded by a satisfied nod from his father as he passed.

"That's a good day's work, son. Are you coming in for your supper?"

"Aye, I've just got this last basket to empty."

He'd filled it over full and couldn't carry it, so he had to drag it to the far end of the field where the stones were being piled ready to be carted away. The sun dipped low on the horizon as he tipped the stones out, and when he straightened up again, he caught sight of something left sitting at the bottom of the basket. He reached in and pulled it out.

It was a small round stone that fitted perfectly into the palm of his hand, its edges smooth to the touch as polished marble. Rab stared at it in surprise. In the centre of the stone was a hole so perfectly round it looked almost like an eye gazing back at him.

Jings! That's an odd wee chunk of rock to find and no mistake! he thought, turning it over in his fingers. *If I was as superstitious as our Cousin Betty, I'd think maybe it was a fairy spyglass left behind when the wee folks danced through the fields at midnight.*

Smiling at the thought, he held it up and put his eye to the hole, looking through the centre of the stone.

The sky seemed to grow darker all of a sudden.

Rab shuddered. He hadn't noticed how red the sinking sun had become. Through the stone, the sky to the west looked bruised and blood-tinged, and the air from the sea held a salty chill. He was just about to drop the stone, when a black-robed figure crossing the fields in the distance caught his attention. He squinted through the hole, trying to make out who it was against the crimson glare of the sun.

The figure was hunched and stooped like an old woman, but there was something unnaturally fast about its movements, as though it was flying across the ground instead of walking. Its clothes flapped in the sudden breeze, fluttering like loose rags in the wind.

Rab felt the cold clawing its way through his shirt all the way to his bones. There was something all wrong about the approaching figure, and he didn't want to stand around waiting to find out what it was. He threw the strange stone as hard as he could, watching in satisfaction as it bounced down the road and disappeared into a ditch. Then he gathered up the baskets and tools and set off across the fields for home.

The sun disappeared as he reached the lane, but he knew his way too well by now to be misled by moonlight. He rounded the corner of the track leading to the farmhouse and stopped dead.

There on the path, blocking his way home, stood an old woman dressed in black.

2

"Betty Davidson! You scared me half to death!" Rab cried, grinning in relief when he recognised the old woman standing before him as his mother's cousin.

"Who'd you expect to see in your lane at this twilight hour—Old Nick himself?" Betty chuckled, drawing her black shawl around her bony shoulders to ward off the chill.

"Dinnae let Pa hear you talk like that, you know he doesnae like it," Rab reminded her as they walked together down the track to the farmhouse. "Are you here to help with the baby? Ma's in sore need of another pair of hands round the house. But why'd you no come earlier when the sun was up? You'll break your legs running across the fields like a wee lassie."

"Eh? Whit are you on about? I've no been—"

"Cousin Betty! You're a rare sight and no mistake!" Agnes came hurrying from the house with two small children in tow. One was in his night shirt and only had one shoe on, and the other was clutching her skirt and crying for his supper. "I was beginning to think you'd no come tonight and I'd be left to deal with this rabble by myself."

"The great general Hannibal was begging his father to let him go to war overseas when he was only nine," Rab teased. "Are you saying you cannae manage a few bairns at the same age?"

"Ordering armies around in far off lands would be a doddle compared to keeping John's fingers out the frying pan and stopping Nannie stabbing herself half to death with her sewing needle!" Agnes snorted. "Och, Willie, will you go and find your other shoe? You'll catch your death of cold!"

"Come away in, dearies, I'll have things set to right in no time," Betty soothed. Her knees creaked as she bent down to lift the youngest boy up, and John snuggled into her neck gratefully, wiping his nose on her shawl.

Agnes was still muttering about 'Hannibal only having to herd elephants and no wee hellions' as she followed Betty in, but the half smile she shot Rab told him he was forgiven for snapping at her earlier. Rab grinned back, glad he wouldn't have to bribe her with his potatoes tonight after all as he was hungrier than a horse.

He went to stow his tools in the barn, then stopped by the pump in the yard to give his arms and neck a quick wash before supper. The wind had picked up, wailing mournfully round the three small buildings that made up their farm. In the dark, the house, barn and byre looked like they were hunched up against the cold. Rab shivered too, remembering the way the figure he'd seen in the twilight had seemed to fly across the ground, and the eerie way its clothes had writhed and clawed at the air like living things.

You're going soft in the head, Rab, he told himself, scrubbing the dirt from under his nails with a wire brush. *It was only Cousin Betty taking a shortcut through the fields. There's more life in her old bones than you give her credit for.*

All the same, Rab was glad to leave the darkness behind and step into the warm glow of firelight inside the house. He barely had time to get his boots off before three small children threw themselves at him, demanding his attention.

"Look, Rab! I've darned all your socks today—aren't the stitches neat? Can I have some of your scone at supper?"

"My shoe! Look, Rabbie, I've found my other shoe!"

"Want my supper! I'm *hungry*!"

Betty stepped in before he was bowled over in a heap. "Nannie, you can show Rab the socks later, go and help Gil set the table. Willie, that shoe would look better on your foot than waving in the air. John, here's a bit of carrot to chew on; supper will be out afore you're finished."

The youngest boy didn't look convinced, but he grabbed the stick of carrot and tottered over to a stool in the corner where he had a good view of Agnes stirring the bubbling pots on the kitchen fire.

Rab took advantage of the temporary calm to take his jacket off and give his mother a kiss on the cheek. She was sitting on the bed set in the wall, feeding the baby and humming softly to her.

"Seeing her so peaceful like that, you wouldnae think she had lungs like the smithy's bellows, would you?" Rab smiled, stroking Isabella's tiny hand.

"She's no even the loudest baby I've ever had," his mother said softly, rocking Isabella back and forth. "That was you, Rab. You think John over there's fixed on nothing but food? When you were a wee lad, you'd howl the place down if you didnae get fed as soon as your belly rumbled."

"He still does," Gil put in, poking Rab playfully with one of the forks he was setting on the table. "You should've heard him bleating on all morning about his empty belly. If Agnes hadnae come with broth, the townsfolk five miles away in Ayr would've heard his whining."

Rab winced, but it wasn't the fork's prongs that hurt him. He saw the way his mother's lips pursed at the thought of her children going hungry, and the way the frown lines in his father's forehead deepened as he hunched over his account books. His parents were doing their best. It wasn't their fault this farm seemed cursed to swallow their toil, and spit back poor seeds in return.

"Take that to the table, Nannie—both hands, mind!" Betty ordered. "No too much, Agnes; it's stew you're doling out, no a bathtub you're filling. Gil, fetch me some more bowls from the dresser. Willie, shoe on *now*, please." The old woman hobbled round the kitchen, marshalling the troops until everything was in its proper place for supper.

When all the children were sitting down, their father said grace, giving thanks for the food that was on the table. Rab was too eager to get started to waste time wishing they had a little more to be thankful for, but Gil didn't have his older brother's tact.

"I'd be more grateful to the Good Lord if there was a wee scrap of meat somewhere in this stew," he muttered, wincing when Rab kicked him under the table.

Their father showed no signs of hearing him, but his choice of topic for supper conversation that night was clearly a reminder there were others worse off than they were.

"How are you boys getting on with that book about India I borrowed from the Ayr Library Society?" he asked Rab and Gil. "Have you finished it yet?"

Gil stared at his half-empty bowl in guilty silence, but Rab nodded. "Nearly, I'm on the last few chapters." It was true he'd turned over most of the pages, but between the exhausting farm work and the baby crying, how much of it he'd managed to take in was debatable.

"You'll be able to find Bengal on the map then?"

"Aye, it's in the north-west of the country, south of the Kathmandu Valley." Rab had looked at the pictures at least, but Gil gawped at his brother like he'd suddenly grown two heads.

"That's right. And do you know whit the news is from there?"

Rab and Gil exchanged glances. They no more knew the latest news from India than the latest news from the moon.

"Well, last year's famine is back and things are worse than afore. There are folks there eating tree bark and grass to fill their bellies. So, we're no doing so badly here, are we?" He pointed to their bowls of boiled potatoes and cabbage, clearly meaning it as an encouragement, but Rab couldn't help feeling it was yet another rebuke.

"I remember when I was a young man of nineteen," their father went on, warming to his subject, "seeing cattle die by the score, and folks clawing through the middens for scraps.

"And when I was no older than wee Nannie there, the stories I heard of the seven-year blight made my hair stand on end! How the harvest was that spoiled by mildew it had to be reaped in midwinter, and how the rotting skins fairly hung off the bones of the sheep in the—"

"Och, William!" their mother interrupted, putting her spoon down with a thump. "That's no a very nice thing for the wee ones to hear."

"Aye, but it's true!"

"That's as maybe, but can we no talk of something a wee bit more jolly afore bed?"

"Whit the bairns want to hear about is the gathering of the witches at Halloween, is that no right?" Betty grinned her gap-toothed smile, and the younger children clapped their hands in delight.

"Aye! Tell us about witches and their curses," Agnes urged.

"And the wee brownies that do work about the house and barns while the tall folk are asleep!" Gil said.

"And the Kelpies that haunt the river crossings on starless nights!" Rab added, eager to hear more of the old woman's stories.

"No tonight," their father said sternly before Betty could open her mouth again. "It's late, and there's a deal of work to be done tomorrow. Get the wee ones to bed, Agnes. Rab and Gil, you help your Ma with the dishes afore you turn in."

Rab groaned inwardly. He'd been hoping for a chance to finish the book on India before bed, but by the time he'd scrubbed the pots out at the pump, he'd be too tired to do more than stumble up to the loft to sleep.

He knew better than to complain as he lugged the

bucket full of dirty bowls and pots into the yard, though. The crescent moon shone down brightly, but its light was cold compared to the warm glow of the kitchen fire through the farmhouse window. Rab rolled up his sleeves and set to work, yelling for Gil to hurry up and bring the hot water before his fingers froze.

His father and Betty appeared at the door before Gil did, the old woman wrapping her black shawl round her shoulders again as she stepped out.

"Will you no stay until morning?" his father urged. "It's a dark night to be walking all the way back to Alloway."

"Och, it's only two miles, and I know the way through the lanes like the back of my hand."

Rab was sure he knew the way even better. Their father hadn't been able to sell their old cottage, so Betty lived there now on her own, keeping the place from falling into disrepair. If he closed his eyes, he could picture every step of the way to the little house where he'd been born.

"Well then, will you no let me take Meg and the cart out to see you home?" said William.

"That old nag?" Betty scoffed. "I thought you'd boiled her up for soup long afore—that's about all she's good for. And you need to keep the other two plough horses fresh for the fields tomorrow," she added quickly before William could renew his offer. "That wee speck of moon up there's like a candle to light my way, and the fairy folk I meet in the lane will keep me company on the road."

"Dinnae talk like that, Betty!" Rab's father frowned. "Some folk round here already think you're a witch without you spouting more of your nonsense!"

Betty just gave a deep-throated chuckle and headed off down the lane, waving to Rab as she passed. His father turned back into the house, but Rab lingered to watch the old woman as she made her way home in the moon's pale light.

A sharp breeze snatched at her shawl, and she hunched her shoulders against the cold, moving as fast as her old bones would carry her. Rab peered at the figure in the darkness, trying to compare it to the black shadow he'd seen crossing the blood-red orb of the setting sun earlier. He wasn't sure, but something about the way the ends of her shawl and bonnet ribbons danced as the wind whipped them made him shudder.

The outline of Cousin Betty in the moonlight looked exactly the same as the shadowy figure he'd seen by the light of the setting sun.

And he was pretty sure the figure he'd glimpsed at sunset had been a witch.

3

"Och, Agnes," Rab sighed. "Is this meant to be porridge you've made, or glue to mend the broken chair?"

"I wish it was glue," Agnes said, throwing him a sour look. "Then maybe it'd stick your teeth together and stop that great tongue of yours from flapping!" She dumped another helping of burnt goo into his bowl and looked ready to smack him over the head with her wooden spoon if he didn't eat it.

Rab opened his mouth to protest, but thought better of it when his mother came in lugging a bucket full of milk from the byre. Despite the baby having another bad night and keeping them all awake, she'd still got up at the crack of dawn to start making cheese skimmings for the market that week. He didn't want to add to her burdens by complaining about his sister falling asleep over by the fire instead of minding the pots. And if he raised his voice any louder, he'd wake the wee ones, and that wouldn't be fair.

Nannie was dozing under the blanket on their parents' wall bed. She was still clutching the half-eaten scone she'd pinched from Rab's supper the night before, when he pretended he wasn't looking. Nannie was the only one Rab let away with that. When Agnes had tried it, he'd nipped her so hard she squealed.

At four and two years old, Wee Willie and John were just about small enough to squeeze together into the trundle bed that pulled out from under the wall bed, but Willie's feet were taking up so much room on John's pillow his younger brother scarcely had room to breathe. The biggest disappointment for Rab when they'd moved here five years ago was that the two-roomed farmhouse wasn't much bigger than their old cottage. If that had been the only problem they faced here, though, he might have been able to chew his thick porridge with better grace.

His father was worried; Rab could tell as soon as he went into the parlour to ask what his day's chores would be. Even Agnes had the sense to tiptoe in from the kitchen for fear of waking the baby, and to set his porridge bowl gently down on his desk. Their father leaned further over his account books, barely glancing at his breakfast. There was another letter added to the pile on the cramped desk, and William Burns kept consulting it, looking at his account books, and back to the letter again. Rab heard the half-eaten porridge gurgle in the pit of his stomach. He knew who the letter was from, and it put him off his food too.

"Are we to go on with clearing that field today, Pa?" Gil asked sleepily, pulling on his boots and trying to stifle a yawn. Their father was so deep in concentration Gil had to ask twice before William heard him.

"Hmph? Whit? No, you'll be with me finishing up ploughing the far fields, Gil. Go and get the horses ready, and I'll be out in a minute."

"Whit about Rab? Is it no his turn for ploughing?"

"He's to go to the smithy to mend that hoe the pair of you broke yesterday."

"Ach, but that's no work, that's a nice wee walk in the morning sun! Could I no—"

"Do as you're told, Gil."

Their father wasn't usually stern with them, but much of his old humour had worn thin with worry and lack of sleep over the last few months.

Gil threw Rab an envious look, giving the door such a hard tug as he closed it behind him it rattled in its frame and woke the baby. Isabella started howling, and Agnes ran to the kitchen to rock her back to sleep. When that didn't help, she took her out into the yard to give their father some peace for his books. When the door was safely closed once more, Rab leaned over his father's desk.

"We're short again this month, aren't we, Pa?" he asked softly so his mother wouldn't hear in the kitchen.

"Aye, that we are, Rab," his father sighed.

"Whit's the factor saying about it? Will he no give us more time?" Rab nodded to the letter his father was holding tightly in his hands. Ever since their kindly landlord had taken to his sickbed a year ago, the estate had been managed for the Fergusson family by a mean-spirited factor, and Rab's father hadn't known a single moment's peace.

"You know that's no Angus McNab's way, son. He wants payment when it's due, and no a day later."

"Will he no take a couple of chickens now, and give us till the end of the week? Ma will have cheese skimmings and eggs for the market on Thursday, and we can make up the rest then."

William's frown turned into a smile of pride. Rab had been keeping his eye on the account books without being asked, just like he'd hoped his eldest son would.

"Aye, that was my thought too. But I've got too much work to do to waste a morning going to the big house at Doonholm to speak to him—the factor spends more time hanging about the Fergussons' kitchens trying to cadge a free meal than he does at his own house. You'll have to stop by when you're going to the smithy."

Rab's father crushed the letter in his hands, his smile turning bitter. Rab didn't like the thought of begging the factor for extra time to pay their rent any better than his father did.

He swallowed his pride, though, and tucked the small

bag of coins his father gave him into his belt for safe keeping.

"Take Meg with you," his father said as he was leaving, "she could do with a bit of exercise. And dinnae forget to get that hoe mended."

Rab didn't need any more reminders that he'd been caught playing on the job the day before. The guilt had cost him even more sleep than the baby's cries and the unsettling image of the figure in the fields he couldn't get out of his head.

He picked a couple of hens from the coop—not the fattest, but not the skinniest either—and tied their feet together before going to fetch Meg from the field behind the barn. The old Clydesdale had once been a fine plough horse, but now her brown hide was flecked with grey and hung in sagging folds round her bones. As soon as she saw Rab she trotted up and nuzzled him in greeting.

"Sorry, old lass, I havenae got an apple for you. But if you'll come to Doonholm with me we might be able to pinch a few from under the factor's nose."

Rab knew the orchards belonged to the Fergusson family, not the tyrant factor, but it gave him a secret thrill to think of stealing anything off the land that Angus McNab was managing. Whether Meg understood him or not, she was willing enough to let Rab saddle her up and tie on the baskets with the broken hoe and chickens, before slowly clomping away with him down the lane.

The mid-October sun had burnt off the morning mist that rose from the River Doon, but small tendrils still wisped their way round the hedgerows as Rab and Meg passed between the fields. Rab couldn't help thinking of his school days, when he and Gil used to run down the hill in the morning, eager to avoid the sting of the tawse across their hands for being late. He'd gladly bear a beating every morning now, if it meant he could still study regularly instead of snatching at bits of arithmetic and grammar in whatever time his father could spare after work.

He was so lost in daydreams of school and learning, he didn't notice at first that Meg's pace had slowed to a crawl.

"Whit's up, lass? You havenae thrown a shoe, have you?"

Rab jumped down and lifted her front leg, looking at the hoof she seemed to be limping on. There, caught between the sole and her iron shoe, was the same round stone he'd found in the fields the day before.

"Ach, this thing? I thought I'd sent it to the bottom of the sheugh," Rab muttered, pulling it out and making sure that this time it did end up at the bottom of the deep drainage ditch at the side of the road.

Before he could get back in the saddle, Meg reared up, swerving away from the ditch. Rab grabbed her reins, looking back to see what had startled her.

It was only then that he realised they were being followed.

Something was coming after them through the fields on the other side of the hedgerow. The morning sun wasn't high in the sky yet, and the far side of the hedge separating the fields from the lane was in deep shadow. Nevertheless, Rab was sure he could make out a figure behind the bramble bushes darting towards them with strange, spider-like movements. The birds had all stopped singing, and in the eerie silence, Rab shivered as he caught a glimpse of trailing black rags through the screen of leaves.

The figure from the day before was back.

And now it was coming for him.

"Gee-up, Meg!" he cried, jumping into the saddle and spurring her into a lopsided canter down the hill.

It's just a trick of the light! he told himself as he urged Meg on faster. *Or it's one of the labourers out in the fields. Or a pedlar come selling ribbons. Or...*

By the time they'd got to the bottom of the hill, Meg was winded, and Rab was out of ways to explain what he'd seen.

No matter. When he finally got up the nerve to turn his head again and look back, the eerie flapping of rags behind the hedge was gone, and the countryside was at peace in the morning glow. Rab sucked in a long breath, then let out a hollow laugh.

"Maybe Gil's right, Meg. Maybe I do have straw for brains."

He jumped down and led the wheezing horse the rest of the way on foot, giving her time to recover. It wasn't long before they came to the sweeping drive that cut through the plantations of the Doonholm estate and led up to the great house itself.

Rab didn't take the main way in, though. His father had been the gardener at Doonholm back when they lived in the old cottage, and Rab knew every winding path and secret glade better than the Fergusson family themselves.

More than that, he knew his way to the orchard.

The apple trees overhung the low fence at the back of the great house, out of sight of the main windows. The crop had been picked, but there were still a few late bloomers growing high up in the branches that Rab could almost reach if he balanced on top of the fence. He tied Meg's reins to a post and clambered up, reaching eagerly for the ripe red apples that hung tantalisingly close to his fingertips.

Agnes is due a wee treat after I've been so bitter to her these last few weeks, he thought, reaching higher. *And the bairns could do with a break from bread pudding on a Sunday. One of Ma's steaming apple pies would be a rare sight on the supper table tomorrow!*

Lost in thoughts of his brothers' and sisters' smiling

faces when he came home with his pockets full of apples, he didn't hear the footsteps behind him until it was too late. A strong hand grasped him by the shoulder, overbalancing him and sending him sprawling to the ground.

"Hey! Whit d'you think you're playing at?" Rab had already demanded, before he rolled over and realised he was staring right at the polished boots of Factor McNab himself.

"Playing at?" the factor snapped, clipping his words like the city gents he was always imitating. "You think stealing is a game, you wee thief?"

"I'm no a thief!" Rab protested, scrambling up and trying to make himself look presentable despite the big smear of mud down one cheek. "I was just... just..."

"Just...?" The factor took a menacing step towards him.

"I'm William Burns's boy, remember?" Rab changed the subject, hoping his father's honesty might do for both of them. "He sent me here with the rent." He pulled the bag of coins out of his belt and held it up to the factor as a peace offering.

"And that's all of this month's rent for Mount Oliphant, is it?" McNab eyed the small bag suspiciously, his beady eyes getting narrower below his ridiculous powered wig.

"Well, most of it. We were hoping you'd take a couple of chickens today, and we'll have the rest in coin by Friday."

Angus McNab eyed the chickens Rab pulled from Meg's saddle baskets in disgust.

"I see. William Burns isnae man enough to come and tell me himself he cannae keep his account books straight, so he sends his thieving wee boy instead with a bribe to buy my favour for another week, is that it?"

The words set off an explosion in Rab's head, like a barrel of gunpowder thrown on a bonfire. His father was a good man, who thought even a monster like Angus McNab would look kindly on a lad bearing gifts. But he hadn't reckoned on just how cold the factor's heart was. Rab's heart burned red hot, though. At the insult to his father, his eyes shot straight from the factor's boots where they'd been fixed in shame right up to his pudgy, beef-fed face. "My father's twice the man you'll ever be, Angus McNab!" he yelled.

"Is that so?" the factor growled. "Well, it's a pity for him his son only has half his wits."

Before Rab could protest further he found himself being dragged by the ear towards the servants' yard at the back of the house. The factor might dress like a dandy instead of the jumped-up farmer he used to be, but his hands had lost none of the steely grip he'd learned from years guiding a plough.

"Ow! Let go! You'll get the rest of your money on Friday!" Rab yelped as he was propelled into the damp scullery that was piled with dirty breakfast dishes.

"And you'll get whit's coming to you. Maybe then you'll learn some manners when talking to your betters," the factor warned, giving Rab's ear one last pinch before letting go. "Morven, teach this boy a lesson. Dinnae let him leave till his thieving hands are scrubbed raw," he ordered. He snatched the purse and chickens Rab was still holding and marched out of the back door, locking it behind him.

Rab turned slowly to see who the factor had been talking to.

Standing in the doorway to the kitchen was a pale-faced ghost of a girl who looked about sixteen, with eyes the colour of pine trees in winter. More striking than her haunting beauty, though, was the crimson blood staining her hands and spattering her apron. The sharp knife she held glittered, and when she parted her white lips, her teeth were bared at him like fangs.

Rab swallowed hard and backed away until he hit the wall.

There was no escape.

4

When Rab's eyes finally adjusted to the gloom of the scullery, he realised that the young maid was actually smiling at him.

"Dinnae let that big bletherskate worry you, he's all wind and no rain," she said, setting her knife on the table and wiping her hands on her apron. "Will you take a wee taste of my bramble pie? It's fresh out the oven."

"Um... aye, that's very kind of—"

Morven disappeared into the kitchen again before he could thank her. He was even more relieved now he'd worked out that the dark stains on her hands and apron were actually smears of blackberry juice and not the evidence of bloody murder.

"There you go, tuck in." The maid came back with a plate and set a steaming slice of fruit pie down on the table in front of him. "The brambles are fresh picked from the bushes up the lane this morning—I gathered them myself."

"You were up in the lane this morning?" Rab asked, his mouth already full of hot pie. "Did you see anyone up there?"

"Who? Farmers and the like?" Morven squinted at him, her green eyes full of cat-like curiosity.

"No, I mean, I thought I saw someone dressed in black following me down the hill."

"Are you no a wee bit young for a sweetheart chasing after you?" the girl laughed, flashing her white teeth again.

Rab's face went bright red, and he blew on a spoonful of pie, pretending it was the heat of the berries that was making him blush. "It looked more like... Ach, never mind me, I'm talking nonsense," he muttered.

Morven leaned against the sink and studied Rab as he ate, until the scraping of his spoon on the plate in the silence started to make him uncomfortable.

"There was one old woman who passed me up there," she said at last, "and she was wearing black. She had an odd look about her as she walked the fields by the hedgerow, like she knew things that were beyond other folks' seeing, you know?"

Rab nodded, even though he wasn't sure what she meant. The girl's eyes darted to the kitchen to make sure they weren't being overhead, then she leaned forward and whispered, "I'm no saying she was a witch, or nothing—that kind of talk can get you into a deal of trouble if you're no careful. But there was something funny about the way her shawl and bonnet strings were flapping around, seeing as there wasnae a breath of wind to stir them. And the terrible things she was muttering under her breath! Well, I've never heard a good Christian woman come out with the like. There was something off about her… I dinnae quite know how to explain it, but she put the very fear of hell into me, and I ran down the hill all the way to the house with my brambles spilling in all directions!"

Rab was leaning forward eagerly now too, the remains of his pie forgotten. "D'you know who she was? The old woman?" he asked.

"No, but when I got back and asked the other maids about it, they said it must've been old Betty Davidson, who lives hereabouts."

Rab drew in sharp breath. "But you dinnae know for sure?" he said. "You didnae see her face?"

"Whit good would that have done me?" Morven shrugged. "I've never seen Betty Davidson afore in my life."

"Eh? How can that be? She lives up the road, at the wee cottage near the old kirk."

"Aye, but I'm no a local," Morven said, getting up to clear his plate away. "I only arrived here myself last night. This is my first day on the job."

She looked like she was ready to go back to work and leave him to his day. Rab wasn't sure why, but there was something in the pale, wistful look of her face that made him want to sit at the table all day talking to her.

"And whit about your folks, where do they come from?" he asked, trying to delay her a bit longer.

"They're... I'm..." Morven's face fell, and she paused for a long moment before she said, "Look, it's no a very happy story, and no worth spoiling the sunshine for. No when there's a late crop of apples out there just waiting to be pinched by a bright lad like yourself." She gave him a sad smile and unlocked the scullery door with the bunch of keys in her apron pocket, ushering Rab out.

"You mean you're no going to make me scrub all these dishes till my knuckles bleed like the factor said?" Rab grinned.

"You keep me from my chores one minute longer, Rab Burns, and I just might," Morven warned, pushing him out into the sunshine and locking the door behind him.

It wasn't until Rab had climbed the orchard fence once more, and was stowing an armful of stolen apples away in Meg's saddle basket, that he realised he'd never told Morven his name.

"Well, how she found that out's a mystery for another day," he said to Meg, urging her down one of the secret pathways through the trees before the factor could catch him for a second time.

It was a three-mile trek in the other direction to the smithy in Purclewan, but Rab couldn't help taking a short detour to see some of his favourite old haunts first.

"We'll only take a wee look at the old kirk," he told

Meg, "and then stop in at the cottage. Betty's no a witch, I'm nearly sure of it, but if she's been talking and acting in a way that makes folks gossip, then she needs to know about it."

When they were back on the open road again, the first landmark that greeted them was the bell tower of the old kirk that gaped empty and abandoned against the sky, half hidden behind the thick trees that circled the churchyard.

A bird burst from one of the overhanging trees, taking flight with a loud cry, and Meg reared up, whinnying in fear. Rab had to bribe her with some of his stolen apples to calm her down again, and even then she refused take a single step into the graveyard.

"Och, you big feartie! You've been listening to too many of Betty's stories," Rab muttered, wrapping her reins round the oak tree guarding the first row of stones. But Meg wasn't the only one who was feeling nervous. A heavy knot of dread had been tied in Rab's stomach when he saw the black-clad figure in the fields. Now it was tightening, sending a shiver up his spine.

It's just the damp, he told himself, pushing the branches aside and stepping carefully past the fallen grave markers. *There's nothing here but broken stones and beetle nests.*

The morning sun didn't seem to penetrate the thick veil of trees, and the mist from the River Doon hung heavy round the remains of the ruined church. Part of the roof had caved in, and the rest was covered in a dense cloak of moss and rotting vegetation. Bramble and thorn branches snaked down from the eaves, clawing at the crumbling kirk walls like grasping fingers. Ivy clambered its way up the cracks and through the broken windows, winding so tightly round the stonework inside that the old kirk looked like it was choking with each breath of wind that stirred the leaves.

Rab gulped. This was no longer the sun-lit place full of late-blooming flowers that he remembered.

He was just turning away to retrace his steps, when something sitting in the doorway of the church caught his eye. Even though the damp mist nipping at his toes was urging him to head straight home, his curiosity got the better of him, and he went over to take a look.

There was a small woven figure lying on the kirk threshold.

When Rab picked it up, he thought at first it was a straw doll, the kind the harvesters would sometimes make for their children. But this one was bigger, and its misshapen dog's body was all wrong. The two ears of straw sticking out on either side of its head were woven to sharp points, and the long tail hanging behind it ended in a knot of thorns. The bottom of the legs where the paws should have been were divided in half on each side, just like the cloven hooves of a goat.

It took Rab a couple of moments more to realise what he held in his hands was a living image of the Devil.

"Lord preserve us!" he yelped, dropping the straw dog and running blindly back through the kirkyard. He tripped over stones and scratched his face on overhanging branches, but he was too frightened to catch his breath till he'd untied Meg and was urging her into a sharp trot back up the road. "Gee-up, Meg! We need to see Cousin Betty and ask her whit she makes of this," Rab panted.

Betty knew everything there was to know about witches and bogles and the spells they cast on unsuspecting village folk. She would know what to make of the straw dog in the kirkyard, and would know what to do next.

Rab pulled on Meg's reins to slow her as they rounded the corner, and the little cottage he knew so well came into view. The whitewash on its walls was chipped and faded, and the thatch on its roof was thin and patchy in places. But to Rab the 'wee clay biggin' that his father had built with his own hands was the equal of all the fancy palaces he read about in India. Even Meg seemed cheered by the sight of the familiar square chimneys puffing out wisps of smoke. She crossed the road, heading to the byre she'd shared for so many years with the milk cows.

"We're no going in there, you daftie," Rab told her. "We're going to see Cousin Betty. Look, there she is sitting in the yard."

He was about to shout over the wall to get the old woman's attention, when he caught sight of what she was doing, and the greeting died on his lips. Betty was sitting on a stool with her back to Rab, her hands moving swiftly over her work. Beside her lay a pile of straw, and in her lap was a small woven figure she was twisting into shape. Rab gave Meg a pat to keep her still while he leaned forward in the saddle, peering at the finished figures standing in a neat row at Betty's feet.

There was a tall one holding what might be a wheat thresher, beside a slightly smaller one in a straw skirt. Next to them were two shorter ones of equal size, holding what looked to Rab like miniature hoes. Then two more smaller ones, each in skirts. Finally, a very short one wearing breeches, and a tiny one that was little more than a bunt of straw representing a young boy.

Rab's eyes widened as he recognised each of the figures.

William Burns and his wife.

Rab and Gil Burns.

Agnes and Nannie.

Wee Willie.

And at the end of the row, the smallest boy, John...

Whit in the name of goodness is Cousin Betty up to? Rab thought, his head spinning. *She's no made corn dollies like that afore! And whit about that nasty piece of work in the kirkyard? That must've been her too!*

He watched in growing horror as Betty finished the last of her figures, holding it up to examine it. The straw glowed like gold in the sunlight, revealing the image of a baby swaddled in a blanket.

It was his youngest sister, Isabella.

All thought of visiting Betty vanished. Rab ducked his head below the wall to stay out of sight, kicking Meg into a fast trot. There was mischief here all right, but it wasn't of the village gossips' making.

The new maid Morven was right.

Betty Davidson was a witch.

5

"Shh, Gil! Stop jiggling around or we'll get caught!" Rab whispered, elbowing his brother in the ribs to get him to sit still.

"Well, you take the handkerchief then!" Gil hissed back. "They keep scuttling about in there and tickling my fingers!"

Rab reached behind his brother's back where he was hiding the handkerchief full of earwigs, careful to hold the knotted ends together and not drop any. Their father shot them a stern look from the end of the pew where he was sitting with their mother and the younger children. Rab brought the piece of linen up to his nose, pretending he was coughing into it. When his father turned his attention back to the minister's sermon, Rab let out a sigh of relief.

"Are you sure this is a good idea, Rab?" Gil whispered. "We'll be in a deal of trouble if Factor McNab finds out whit we're up to."

"Aye, that big birkie who thinks he's lord of all the tenant farmers round here deserves everything that's coming to him," Rab muttered. "Now hold your tongue and wheesht! Wait for the prayers like we planned."

Gil sat back and pretended to listen to Reverend Dalrymple, who was still spouting forth from the pulpit. Rab, however, fixed his eyes on the powdered wig in the pew right in front of him. He hadn't forgotten what Factor McNab had said about his father, and all the stolen apples in Scotland wouldn't make up for his hurtful words.

Just you wait, McNab, Rab thought darkly. *Just you wait.*

Keeping the cloth full of earwigs hidden until prayer time wasn't the only thing Rab had to worry about. Checking to make sure his father didn't have his eye on him, and his mother's attention was on the sleeping baby, Rab turned his head and studied the congregation sitting on the pews behind him. The simple church was packed with farmers, day labourers, and their families, all wearing their Sunday best. Fine families like the Fergussons had their own pew stalls at the front, but the poorer folk sat towards the back, making way for their betters.

Right at the far end of the church, on the pew nearest the door, sat Betty Davidson. She wasn't listening to the minister either. She was staring at the girl a few rows ahead of her. Betty wasn't the only one whose eyes were fixed on the Fergussons' new maid. Some of the young men were nudging each other and whispering behind their hands, paying no more attention to Reverend Dalrymple's sermon than farmers paid to the bleating of their sheep.

Morven's dark hair was hidden beneath a neat white cap, but the sun from the high windows glinted on the curls that escaped, giving them a sheen like polished mahogany. Her green eyes were narrowed in concentration as she took in every word the minister was saying, her pale hands folded in her lap as though she was praying. She looked like a picture of a saint Rab had seen in a book once, as if she was weighed down with sorrows, but was too good a soul to burden others with her troubles.

I hope I get a chance to talk to her again soon, he thought. *Then maybe she'll tell me her sad story and I can help somehow. Maybe then she'll tame that smile of hers and it'll be a bit less wild.*

Rab wouldn't forget in a hurry what an idiot he'd been when he'd first seen her white teeth in the gloom of the scullery and thought she was baring a set of fangs at him.

Whit a mistake to make! he thought. *But then I'm more used to folk having teeth like Cousin Betty over there.*

Betty Davidson was an old woman, and a plain one at that. Her nose was hooked, and her pointed chin jutted from her deeply lined face like a rocky crag on the coastline. When she laughed, the few teeth she had left wobbled in her gums, and her grey eyes were cloudy from years spent hunched over cooking fires. She wasn't a pretty picture like Morven, but up until now Rab had always welcomed the sight of her coming up the lane to their farmhouse, and had looked forward to evenings spent sitting round the fire while she spun her strange tales of the supernatural.

Now Rab wasn't sure what to think.

Is she a witch, or is she no? he wondered, wishing there was an easy answer to the question. *Maybe the corn dollies are no for a wicked purpose after all. Maybe it wasnae her I saw coming for me in the fields. Maybe—*

"Rab! Will you stir yourself? It's prayer time," Gil hissed, kicking him so hard under the pew Rab nearly dropped his insect-filled handkerchief.

Best to come straight out with it and ask Betty after church, Rab decided, getting to his feet with the rest of the congregation and putting his hands together in prayer. *Then she can explain it all and I'll no keep worrying about it.*

He had a more pressing job to attend to right now, though. While the Reverend intoned his prayer, and the rest of the congregation stood with their eyes closed and their hands clasped, Rab undid the knotted ends of the handkerchief, shaking its contents out onto the starched collar of the man in the pew in front of him. There was a flurry of grey legs and waving antennas on the white linen, and Rab and Gil held their breath, waiting to see if their plan would work.

The earwigs scuttled about, looking for a dark place to hide from the beams of sunlight streaming through the windows. One found the bottom of the factor's wig and disappeared under. That was all it took. The rest quickly followed, and within moments Angus McNab was dancing around like the minister was playing the fiddle instead of reading the benediction.

Rab and Gil bit back their grins as they watched the action through half-closed eyes, trying to keep their faces as straight as they could while the factor jerked and scratched.

A pompous man like him would no more take his wig off in public than a woman would go to a ball in her nightgown, so he was stuck trying to fight off the itching till the minister finished talking and released the congregation.

There were a lot of sideways looks and a few giggles as the factor jiggled and hopped, waiting impatiently as the people filed slowly from the pews and made their way to the door.

But William Burns had his eyes on Rab instead as they headed down the aisle behind the squirming factor, and he raised his eyebrow at his son accusingly.

Rab gave him an innocent shrug and stuck his hands in his pockets, making a mental note to shake the handkerchief out on the way back home in case his mother found any guilty traces of insect legs when she washed it.

The people nearest the door stepped back to let the minister and the Fergusson family pass through, then the gap closed again as the factor approached.

"Let me pass!" he commanded, pushing his way through the crowd instead of waiting his turn. Rab's hands clenched into fists in his pockets, and he had to grit his teeth to stop himself from saying something out loud about McNab's rude behaviour.

It always annoyed him the way that folk with money acted like they were so superior simply because they had fine clothes and ate beef instead of haggis.

For all the tinsel and baubles he wore, a man like Angus McNab wasn't any better than the rest of them underneath.

Half out of his mind with itching, the factor gave up any pretence of patience and shoved past the last two people in his way to get to the door, knocking one of them over as he ran outside and hurried down the road.

"Hey! Watch whit you're doing!" Rab yelled after him, rushing over to help the old woman up. It didn't matter to him that he'd spent the whole service wondering if Betty Davidson was a witch, not now she was sprawled on the flagstones clutching her wrist and wincing in pain.

"Here, lean on my shoulder," Rab said, helping her slowly to her feet.

"Pox-ridden son of a she-goat!" Betty muttered behind McNab's fleeing back. "I hope you choke on your fine beef dinner and it stops your heart dead, you mean wee—"

"Ssh! We're in a church, Cousin Betty!" Rab reminded her. The old woman had a sharp tongue, and this was no place to be exercising it.

There was a much larger crowd of young men gathered round the other person McNab had shoved. Even though she hadn't fallen down or hurt herself, there were so many arms extended to help Morven that it looked like she was surrounded by the spokes of a giant cartwheel.

"Vain wee minx," Betty growled. "She's no worth the air she's breathing. The Fergussons ought to keep a close eye on that one."

Morven turned as she was escorted out by two of the young farmers who'd managed to claim an arm each, and she threw Betty a curious look, half-question, half-challenge.

Betty scowled back, muttering darkly under her breath.

"Peace, Betty," Rab's father warned, taking her by the shoulder and sitting her down on a pew to check her wrist for fractures. "You'll no make any friends by showing your jealousy to the whole congregation. The girl cannae help her good looks, but you're in charge of your tongue, and you can swallow those sinful words of yours afore they come out, if you've a mind to."

That put Betty in a sour mood, and no mistake.

She refused to be taken to see Doctor Campbell and insisted on going straight back to the cottage. She wouldn't let the family cook dinner for her either, and shut the door behind her with curt thanks when they walked her home. She didn't even invite them in to warm their feet by the fire.

It's almost as if she's got something to hide in there, Rab thought as they tramped back up the hill to Mount Oliphant.

His former suspicions began to return, and by the time he and Gil had done their afternoon chores, finished their arithmetic lesson with their father, and helped lay the table for supper, the knot of apprehension was starting to tighten in his stomach again. Even Gil's whispered jokes about the way Angus McNab had danced a jig in front of the whole congregation couldn't help him shake the feeling that something was wrong.

When his mother placed a steaming apple pie down on the table for pudding, Rab felt certain he was going to have to pay for his thieving somehow in the days to come.

"And you're sure the Fergussons were happy to let you

have the apples?" his father asked him before cutting the first slice. All eyes at the table turned to him, and Rab felt his cheeks grow hot.

"Och, William, leave the lad alone. You know the Provost didnae grudge us a few apple pies when you were working for him," Rab's mother said, coming to his rescue.

"Aye, but now that he's too sick to manage the estate and Angus McNab is in charge, we cannae risk taking a single blade of grass from the orchard without permission."

At the mention of the factor's name, Gil started giggling so hard he had to go outside and catch his breath before he could eat his apple pie. Their father raised an eyebrow at Rab again, but Rab pretended he was too busy shovelling pastry into his mouth to notice.

After supper, when John, Willie and Nannie were dozing in the older children's laps, their father opened a bible to read to them before bed.

"I thought we'd take a look at Proverbs eighteen," he said, drawing the candle closer as he turned the well-worn pages.

"Is that the one about being sheltered from greedy and arrogant enemies?" Gil asked, trying to make up for his fit of giggles earlier with a show of cleverness. "After whit Factor McNab did to Cousin Betty, that's a good one to end the day on."

"No, son," William shook his head. "That's Psalm

nineteen you're thinking of. Proverbs eighteen is about how to get along with other people." He shot his three eldest children a meaningful look, and Rab and Gil exchanged guilty glances.

Their father began reading, and Agnes and Gil, eager to show their father they were paying attention, hushed the two young boys on their laps and listened hard to his words. Rab tried to attend closely too, but Nannie was curled up warm and heavy against his chest, her soft breathing making him sleepy as he stared into the fire.

The flames seemed to dance in the grate as a puff of wind blew down the chimney, reminding him of Angus McNab jerking and hopping about as he scratched his head in church that morning. Then he remembered what Betty had muttered under her breath.

It had sounded like a curse.

Suddenly his father's words grew louder, as though calling him back from the brink of sleep. A coal popped and hissed, the flames leaping higher, and Rab flinched, nearly tipping Nannie onto the floor.

"Did you catch that last line, Rab?" their father asked, seeing his son's eyes fixed on the fire.

"Um... can you read it again? The shifting coals startled me."

"Aye, verse twenty-one was: *'Death and life are in the power of the tongue: and they that love it shall eat the fruit thereof.'*"

The rest of his father's words faded as Rab blinked at the flickering fire.

Death and life are in the power of the tongue...

And what was it Betty had muttered under her breath when Angus McNab pushed her over in his haste to get out of the church?

'I hope you choke on your fine beef dinner and it stops your heart dead.'

Rab swallowed hard.

If Betty Davidson really was a witch, the factor might not have long to live.

6

The autumn mornings were growing darker.

The sun had risen pale and sickly, and the skies were slate grey above the field where Rab was clearing the last of the stones. The cold nipped at his fingers all morning as he levered up rocks with his hoe and dragged his basket over to the road to be emptied onto the growing pile. By midday, the sweat running down his back felt like fingers of ice tickling his skin, and he was starting to wish he'd drawn the short straw and spent the morning mucking out the byre instead of Gil.

Gathering the dung might be a stink of a job, but at least the cows keep the byre warm, he thought.

He yawned and stretched, wishing he'd been able to get more sleep. But it wasn't Isabella who had kept him tossing and turning the night before. Betty Davidson's words from the church had been echoing round his head, chased by the Bible verse his father had read. By the time they'd finally stopped their game of tag and given him peace, the cock was already crowing and Agnes was getting up to milk the cows.

Maybe if I paid more attention to my work, my head wouldnae be so full of strange thoughts, he told himself as he dragged his final load of rocks across the field. *I'll help Pa with the threshing this afternoon, that'll... Hey! Whit's this?*

Rab bent down, picking up the stone that had slipped from the overfull basket. It was smooth and round, with a large circular hole in the middle.

"Whit the—?"

Rab stared at it in amazement.

It was the same one he'd thrown away twice already.

He turned the stone over in his hands, puzzled by the sight of it. Its polished surface reminded him of pebbles he found at the coast on summer trips to the sea. It hadn't been rounded by a workman's wheel and the hole in the centre was too big to have been made by a chisel. It was an uncanny thing; shaped by nature, yet somehow not altogether natural.

With a heavy sense of foreboding, Rab lifted the stone to his eye and looked through it. At once the skies turned dark as a storm-tossed sea, thick clouds rolling in from the east and colliding in a swirling mass above him.

Lighting flashed down, tearing at the air as it snaked to the ground. Thunder shook the earth, the stone vibrating in his hand with each aftershock. Its polished surface turned icy cold, and he fought the urge to drop it and run from the dreadful sight. Somehow, he was rooted to the spot, watching helplessly as something else began to appear in the raging sky.

Black shapes were emerging from behind the clouds, flitting across the sky like monstrous ravens. But these were no birds. Gulping down his fear, Rab gripped the stone tighter, catching glimpses of ghostly figures dressed in tattered rags that fluttered wildly in the wind. They seemed to be flying, but as one swooped lower, Rab finally saw what it was holding.

The creatures were riding on broomsticks.

There was another flash of lighting, and the closest figure turned its head. Rab gasped in horror: he'd been spotted. Suddenly the figure wheeled in the sky, rushing towards him in a blaze of lightning and a furious flapping of black rags.

"Rab!"

A hand clamped down on his shoulder, and Rab jumped in fright, nearly dropping the stone.

"Whit have you got there?" Agnes demanded.

Rab blinked, his hand closing tightly over the stone. The sky was back to normal, the turbulent clouds replaced by the glimmer of weak sunlight through the wash of dreary grey.

The sinister figures were gone.

"Nothing," he muttered. "I was just..."

Agnes eyed him suspiciously, then tossed her head. "Fine, keep your secrets. Are you coming in for dinner?

Ma's got a pot of soup on. Nannie helped make it, so I'm no saying it's up to much, but you'd best come and get it while it's hot."

"Right. I'll be there in a wee minute."

Rab made a show of gathering up his hoe and basket so Agnes would go on ahead of him, then he stared at the sinister object in his hand. There was something wicked held inside that circle of stone; he could feel it. Betty had often talked of witches gathering at Halloween, and he'd always thought she was making up the stories to amuse them. Now, after all the odd things he'd seen, he began to wonder if she hadn't been boasting instead.

It wasn't long now till Halloween, and he'd seen Betty making preparations in the yard. If what he'd glimpsed in the stone was real—and not some vision brought on by overwork or lack of sleep—then Betty's stories might actually be true.

All Hallows Eve was almost upon them, and the witches were gathering.

Rab grasped the stone firmly and strode back to the farmhouse, determined to rid himself once and for all of the stench of witchery that had been following him. Glancing round the yard to make sure the rest of the family were out of sight, Rab stopped by the duck pond, and threw the stone in with all his might. It hit the centre, the sudden splash scattering the ducks and sending them flapping and squawking into the air. Rab watched the stone sink, disappearing under the deep green murk of weeds and moss at the very bottom.

That'll be the last I see of the weird sights that cursed lump of rock holds, he thought in relief.

He tried not to dwell on the troubling vision as he ate his broth and chatted to his mother about her plans for going to the market later that week. Between guarding his hunk of bannock against Agnes's creeping fingers, and keeping Willie and John amused with stories of the buried treasure to be found out in the fields, Rab's mood had lifted by the time lunch was over and he had to go back to work.

"Will I come and help you thresh in the barn this afternoon, Pa?" he asked.

"No, son, we'll leave that till tomorrow. I've a notion that the rain's no far off, and I want to get that back field tilled afore it arrives. Your Ma's got an errand she wants you to run." His father didn't look too pleased about it, and he threw his wife a disapproving look.

"Ach, away, William, it's only Christian charity," Rab's mother said. "I'll no have Betty going hungry on account of Angus McNab's bad manners."

"Whit do you need me to do?" Rab asked, his heart already sinking when he saw his mother ladling soup into a broth bottle and packing up a loaf of bannock bread.

"Take this to Cousin Betty for me, Rab. With that

wrist of hers she'll no be up to much cooking."

"Och, Ma," Agnes complained, "you said I could take it!"

"You can go with him, Aggie," their mother sighed, eager to avoid starting a war between her eldest son and daughter. "But your father's right, it'll be raining afore supper, and I dinnae want you caught in it and catching your death. Meg's too big for you to handle on your own, so Rab can take you both down on her."

Rab and Agnes exchanged unenthusiastic glances. Rab wasn't sure Meg would get them there and back much faster than they could walk, but the thought of visiting Cousin Betty alone after everything he'd seen made him almost glad of his annoying sister's company.

As he suspected, Agnes fussed and fretted all the way down to the cottage, wriggling about in the saddle behind him and complaining he was taking up too much room. Rab let her prattle on without checking her, keeping in mind what his father had said the night before about getting on better with others. If Agnes was sore with him, he only had himself to blame for being mean to her for the last few months.

I should've given her some of my bannock, he thought, feeling guilty. *It's no fair I'm always treating Nannie to wee extras and no giving Agnes so much as the time of day. It's no my food she wants, it's attention she's after.*

With Rab biting his tongue every time Agnes complained, they managed to make it all the way to

Alloway without falling out. But the peace only lasted until they dismounted and were standing on the doorstep ready to knock.

"We'll no go in, Agnes," Rab said, the hair on the back of his neck prickling. "We'll just drop her dinner off and be on our way."

"Eh? Whit are you talking about? Betty cannae do much with that arm of hers. We'll go in and help her straighten the place and make her something for her supper while we're here."

"That's no a good idea." Rab shook his head.

"Why no?" Agnes demanded.

Because I think she might be a witch, and I'm starting to fear her, Rab thought. He didn't have enough faith in his own conclusions to say that out loud, though, so he said instead, "Because Ma doesnae want us caught in the coming downpour, that's why."

"Och, away!" Agnes snorted, giving the door a sharp rap with her knuckles. "We'll no drown in a wee drop of rain, you big daftie!"

Before Rab could argue further, the door swung open, and Morven came marching out, her green eyes blazing and her teeth clenched in anger. She tripped over the children's feet on the doorstep, and Rab had to grab hold of her arm to stop her tumbling down.

"Let the wee minx go, Rab!" Betty said, charging out behind her like she was chasing rats from a barn. "A mouthful of dirt's the very thing she deserves."

"Whit's going on?" Rab gasped, looking from one angry face to the other in confusion.

"Your cousin's an ungrateful old goat, that's whit's going on!" Morven muttered, righting herself and glaring at Betty. "I was only trying to help."

"You've done enough mischief as it is. I'm no wanting any part of it." Betty scowled, throwing a small poultice bag at Morven, who caught it before it hit the ground.

"I made it up to help your sore wrist," Morven protested. "It's my mother's recipe. She always used to make up a plaister and poultice when I was wee and scabbed my knees, or..." Morven's bottom lip trembled, and she turned her face away so the old woman wouldn't see the tears welling in her eyes.

"Is she gone?" Rab asked softly. "Your ma, I mean?"

Morven nodded, and swallowed hard. "And my pa and the wee bairns too. Peggy was about your sister's age when the fever took them from me. She had the same dark eyes and all." Morven's frown softened as she gazed at Agnes, and a wistful smile of remembrance flitted across her pale lips. "You're a pretty wee thing and no mistake, just like my Peggy was. Whit's your name, pet?"

Agnes beamed at Morven. It was the first time in ages anyone had said anything to her that wasn't an order to get her work done or to keep out of their way while they did theirs. It was certainly the first time she could remember anyone calling her pretty. "I'm Agnes," she smiled. "Are you the new maid at Doonholm? Everyone's been talking about you. Ma says half the farmers in Ayrshire want to marry you, even the ones who have wives already!"

"Och, dinnae listen to that nonsense." When she smiled back, Morven's eyes narrowed in the cat-like way Rab had seen before in the scullery, and her voice took on a soft purring note that showed she was pleased at his sister's words despite her protests. She reached out and stroked Agnes's coarse brown hair that hung in a shaggy ponytail down her back. "My Peggy had hair exactly like yours. You two could've been twins."

"That's enough of that!" Betty snapped, jerking Morven's hand back.

"Ow!" Agnes yelped, clutching at her head as some strands of hair were pulled loose by Morven's fingers. "Watch whit you're doing, Cousin Betty!"

It was Morven who apologised, though. "Sorry, Agnes, I didnae mean to hurt you."

"It was no your fault," Agnes muttered, scowling at her cousin.

Betty ignored her and held out a hand to Morven. "Give them back," she demanded.

"Whit?" Morven blinked.

"The hairs you took, you wee thief. Give them back right now!"

Rab and Agnes stared at her in amazement. Cousin Betty was clearly going soft in the head.

"Come away in, Cousin Betty, I've brought some soup for you," Agnes soothed, taking Betty by the shoulders and hustling her into the cottage. "Are you coming, Rab?"

"In a minute, I'm going to put Meg in the byre first," Rab called. The old horse would've been just as happy tied up by the front door and lunching on the flowerpots, but Rab wanted an opportunity to talk to Morven alone.

"Sorry about her," Rab said when the front door closed. "I dinnae know whit's got into Cousin Betty recently, she's been acting awfy strange."

"Aye, so folks have been saying," Morven agreed. "She needs to be careful, Rab. I've only been here a few days, and the stories I've been hearing about her are..."

"Are whit?" Rab urged.

"Ach, sorry, I dinnae have time to stop and talk now, I only came by on my way from the doctor's to drop in a wee poultice. I thought it might bring down the swelling in Betty's wrist."

"The doctor? You're no sick, are you?" Rab asked in alarm.

"No me, it's the factor," Morven said. "He took ill over dinner yesterday with the Fergussons, and he was carried up to one of the guest bedrooms as he was too poorly to stand the journey home. Doctor Campbell's been with him ever since. The doctor sent me over to his house to collect some more supplies, so I've got to hurry back." Morven showed him the basket she was carrying and started off down the lane.

A sudden suspicion made Rab call her back. "Wait! Whit happened to the factor at dinner?"

"He choked on a slice of beef and collapsed. The doctor thinks it's a heart attack. I've got to get back, Rab, I really must." Morven turned and started running towards Doonholm.

Rab stood frozen to the spot, staring at her in horror.

'Death and life are in the power of the tongue...' His father's words echoed in his head, followed by Betty's voice muttering under her breath, *'I hope you choke on your fine beef dinner and it stops your heart dead.'*

7

"Whit did Betty give you, Agnes?" Rab demanded, flicking the reins to make the strong plough horse hitched to the cart jog on faster. "Show me."

Agnes shifted uncomfortably on the seat beside him, refusing to look him in the eye. "I told you, she didnae give me anything. You're going daft and imagining things."

But Rab knew he hadn't imagined Cousin Betty whispering to Agnes before they left her cottage the other day, handing her two small bundles wrapped in brown paper. He'd seen Agnes shove them into the pocket of her dress, but since then, she hadn't let him close enough to find out what she'd hidden there. She even sat on the other side of the table at mealtimes so he couldn't reach into her pocket, and that made him more suspicious than ever. If Agnes was hiding something so important she'd rather give up the opportunity to pinch food off his plate than have him discover what it was, then he needed to find out her secret, fast.

"I can always tell when you're lying to me, Agnes

Burns," Rab said sternly. "Your face goes all red and pinched like a wizened apple, and you smell even fishier than a smoked haddock from—"

"Och, leave the lass alone, Rab," their mother called from the back of the cart. "She's no doing anyone any harm. We'd get to market a deal safer if you'd just concentrate on the road. These eggs need to get there fresh, no half scrambled with the way you're cracking those reins."

"Sorry, Ma." Rab loosened his grip on the leather, easing the plough horse into a walk once more as they reached the main road leading into Ayr. Even with Factor McNab sick and not breathing down their necks for the rest of the rent, they couldn't afford to arrive in the market square with broken eggs and overturned milk urns.

The road was crammed with carts on their way to market, their drivers trying to avoid running down the housewives carrying baskets of fresh bread. Adding to the crush were farmers herding sheep and cattle, and street sellers with their packs of cloth and ribbons. With Agnes cradling Isabella up front and their mother holding tight to the precious urns and baskets in the back, Rab didn't trust the skittish horse with the reins alone, so he jumped down and led them the rest of the way, pushing through the crowds till they came to the market square.

Even though it was still early, the market was already full, and Rab had to walk the length of the square to find a free stall to set up their farm produce. Fresh eggs, cheese skimmings and butter were always in high demand in the town, and he knew it wouldn't take long before his mother sold their small supply. Even so, he couldn't help pacing restlessly as he waited for their regular customers to arrive. His mind was racing, thoughts of Factor McNab taking ill so suddenly after Cousin Betty's terrible curse all mixed up in his head with memories of her woven dolls and the menacing image of the Devil he'd found in the old kirk.

In his mind's eye, he could still clearly see the flapping rags of the witches he'd glimpsed through the stone, and the whirling pictures in his head were making him dizzy. He didn't realise he was walking in circles round the stall and muttering to himself until he tripped over a milk urn and nearly sent its contents spilling across the cobbles. Luckily, his mother caught it in time, but the look she gave him was reproach enough.

"I dinnae know whit's got into you these last few days, Rab," she tutted, "but you're no use to me with your head in the clouds. Go for a wee walk and come back when you've settled."

"How come he gets let off work when he cannae be bothered?" Agnes went red in the face with the unfairness of being left holding the baby and counting change at the same time. "I havenae had a chance for a wee jaunt about town since afore Isabella came along!"

"Then go with him, Aggie," Mrs Burns sighed. "Dinnae go far, and stay out of trouble. I'll mind the stall, but if the baby starts crying bring her straight back."

Rab wasn't sure if their mother was taking pity on Agnes, or just needed a break from her children for a few minutes' peace. Either way, he wasn't thrilled at being stuck with two younger sisters to keep an eye on when he already had so much on his mind. Agnes was determined not to get left behind, though, and grabbed hold of his arm with the free hand that wasn't wrapped round the baby.

"Where are we off to, then?" she demanded.

"Let's take a turn about town and go down to the Wallace Tower," Rab said, steering her through the crowds.

They weaved their way down High Street to the corner of Mill Vennel, where they came to the old baronial tower whose clock was striking nine. They sat down on a low wall, watching the townsfolk and famers passing by, each with their own stories written in the lines on their faces or in the rich cut of the cloth they wore.

I wonder if I'll ever get a chance to tell the stories of the town and the townsfolk? Rab wondered, remembering how he used to love scribbling rhymes in the margins of his schoolbooks back when he'd been a young scholar at Alloway. The teacher hadn't been best pleased at the vandalism, but he hadn't discouraged Rab either, and even gave him extra lessons in verse after class. Rab missed the chance to write his poems about the people and places he saw, almost as much as he missed the easier life he'd had in the old cottage at Alloway.

"It's funny, is it no?" Agnes said, breaking into his thoughts.

"Whit?" Rab muttered.

"Wee Isabella. She willnae sleep at night when the house is as quiet as the grave, but bring her to the bedlam of town, and all the rumbling carts and bellowing cattle in Ayr cannae keep her from snoring."

Rab looked down to see Isabella fast asleep in the crook of her big sister's arm, and felt a pang of jealousy. He couldn't remember the last time he was so carefree he could sleep that peacefully.

"Hey! Look at that!" Agnes cried suddenly, jerking the baby awaking without meaning to as she jumped up.

"Whit now?" Rab demanded.

"Can you no smell it?" Agnes pointed to the basket held by the baker's boy standing on the corner. "There's sweet cakes in there, and sugar fingers and all!"

Rab could almost see his sister's mouth watering, and he knew trouble was brewing.

"We'd best get back. You've gone and woken the baby, and she'll be wanting Ma to feed her now."

"But, *Rab*..." Agnes protested, digging her heels in when he tried to lead her away.

"If we've no got the money to pay our rent, how are we meant to pay for treats, Aggie, hmm?" he growled. "Come on."

Agnes wouldn't budge. "You do odd jobs for the other farmers and help the smithy when he's repairing our tools, and I *know* they dinnae pay you with bannock bread for your trouble," Agnes scowled. "You always have a wee stash of coins, Rabbie Burns, and I've seen you sneak wee tidbits to Nannie and Willie and John after market day afore. Last week I saw them with a sugared almond each! You never get me anything nice, so can you no treat me just this once? *Please*, Rab? Just one sugar bun, and I'll share it with you and Isabella, and even keep a bite for the wee ones."

Rab felt his heart sink to his boots. It was true he did odd jobs for a few meagre pennies, but anything he earned went straight into his father's purse to pay the rent. He didn't want to admit that the small treats he snuck to the younger children were pinched whenever a baker or stall holder's back was turned.

"You're halfways to being a woman now, and too old to be whining over things you know we cannae afford," he snapped, his guilt making him sound harsher than he meant to. "Your racket's got poor wee Isabella screaming herself blue. Come on, we need to get her back to Ma."

"That's all you ever care about!" Agnes stamped her foot, making the baby cry even harder. "Isabella and John and Willie and Gil, and your precious wee Nannie who gets half your dinner instead of the smacks you dole out to me! You wouldnae care if I was dead in a ditch and you had one less sister! If you're so worried about the baby, then *you* take her to Ma. I'm off to find myself a better family and a kinder big brother than you'll ever be!"

Agnes thrust Isabella at Rab and went marching off, her boots kicking up dust as she stomped across the cobbles.

"Agnes! Come back, it's no safe to go running off," Rab yelled. Blind with fury, Agnes was straying right into the path of the rumbling carts drawn by heavy plough horses and monstrous bullocks. With the crying baby in his arms, he couldn't go chasing after her, though. "Agnes!" he called again, trying to get her attention.

She turned to scowl at him, and he hoped she'd seen sense and was going to come back.

Then his blood froze in horror.

Agnes tripped on the uneven cobbles, tumbling headfirst into the path of an oncoming cart drawn by two enormous Clydesdales. The driver was too busy munching on his hunk of bread and cheese to notice the girl sprawled right in front of his horses' plunging hooves. Any second now, there was going to come a horrible collision and a sickening crunching of bones. Rab could only swallow the scream that was rising in his throat and turn his face away at the last moment.

He didn't see what happened next.

8

The next thing Rab knew, a crowd of people had gathered round him. A kindly old woman took Isabella from his arms, and a labourer helped him sit on the kerb before his knees gave out beneath him.

"Give the lad some room," the man ordered. "He's feeling faint."

"Agnes!" Rab called, trying to see through the press of people to the road. "My sister!"

"She's fine, Rab," a familiar voice in the crowd said. "She just skinned her knee is all."

Rab looked up to see Morven the maid helping Agnes limp onto the pavement next to him. His sister's face was pale and there was a gash on one leg, but her bones looked intact, and her head wasn't squashed flat like Rab had been expecting.

"Whit?" he gasped.

"You're a brave one, and no mistake!" Someone in the crowd patted Morven on the back.

"Aye! Did you see the way she jumped in front of the horses and pulled the wee lassie away in the nick of time?" another farmer chimed in.

"I've never seen anyone move so fast in my life!"

"No fast enough," a woman said, passing a basket through the crowd. Delicately sewn handkerchiefs had been hastily bundled back inside, and the fine lace edging was covered in mud. "You'll no be selling them today I'm afraid, lass."

Morven took the basket with a rueful smile, selecting the least soiled handkerchief and tying it in a neat bow round Agnes's cut leg.

"Ach, no!" Agnes tried to stop her. "Dinnae waste your fine linen on me!"

"If they're good enough for rich ladies to blow their noses on, they're more than good enough for your sore knee," Morven smiled. "Anyway, a sweet wee thing like you deserves pretty things."

Agnes beamed at the maid through her tears, and Rab had to fight the urge to hug them both in front of the crowd of onlookers who were gawping at them. Instead, he asked, "Where's the baby? Did someone take her?"

Agnes rolled her eyes and scowled at him. "I'm fine, Rab, thanks for asking."

Before he could tell her what a scare he'd got and how glad he was she was safe, the old lady passed back the crying baby, whose face was wrinkled up like a prune with howling.

"Aw, poor wee thing." Morven took her from Rab

before he could protest, rocking her back and forth. As the crowds lost interest and began to disperse, Morven began to hum a soft tune. Isabella opened her eyes and stared up at the maid, her cries fading as she listened to the soothing song. Rab could only watch in surprise as Isabella snuggled into the crook of Morven's neck, lulled to sleep again before she had even finished singing.

"You've got a real way with wee ones," he said, shaking his head in amazement. "Even Ma cannae get her to settle that quick."

"I had a lot of practice with my own wee brothers and sisters," Morven said, "before..." She trailed off, her smile fading. "Let's get you back to your ma," she told Agnes. "She'll be worried if she hears the news that a lassie near got run over in the High Street. Rab, can you help her while I take the baby?"

Rab was trying to check Agnes over for any bruises or broken bones, but his sister kept smacking his hand away, same as he did to her every time she tried to pinch from his supper plate. He was beginning to think he deserved the scowl she was giving him. If he'd been a better big brother, none of this would've happened.

"Put your arm round my neck, and I'll help you walk," he offered. But Agnes pushed him away, clinging on to Morven's free arm and limping with her down the street. Rab was left to follow behind carrying Morven's basket. His relief at his sister's rescue turned to a twinge of jealousy when he saw the adoration in her eyes as she gazed up at Morven. Agnes used to look at him like that.

Not anymore.

When they reached the market square, their mother was packing the empty baskets and urns into the cart. She turned to give them a tongue-lashing for lateness, but when she saw the way Agnes was limping and the bloody handkerchief tied round her leg, the sharp words died on her lips.

"Whit in the name of goodness happened?" she gasped.

"I nearly got run down in the road, Ma, and Morven saved me from being crushed to death by cart horses! She was *amazing*!" Agnes gushed. "We've been talking, and now that Cousin Betty's got a sore arm and cannae help round the house, maybe Morven can come instead and help with the wee ones? Please, Ma? I've only got one good leg now, and Rab's no use at all with the housework, so an extra pair of hands would be a good thing, d'you no think?"

Rab opened his mouth to protest. He did more work than the rest of his siblings put together, but Agnes wasn't about to let him get a word in edgeways.

"She's *so* good with the baby—she can get her to sleep just with singing. Look! You'd think Isabella had been snoring all morning instead of screaming her head off this half hour."

"Well... another pair of hands would be a great deal of use," their mother smiled. "But I'm sure you've got more than enough work to do at the big house as it is, do you no, Morven?"

"Och, they've got more servants at Doonholm than they know whit to do with," Morven laughed. "I thought I'd be worked to death, but I've even got time in the evenings to sew my handkerchiefs for market."

She showed their mother the basket full of linen. Even covered in dust and mud, the work was exquisite.

"Aw, and you ruined them fetching my daft wee lass out of the road," Mrs Burns frowned. "I'm so sorry."

"I'd chuck a whole cartload in the river if it saved one hair on this wee lassie's head." Morven smiled her cat-like smile again, stroking Agnes's cheek. "Or this bonnie baby, for that matter—she's adorable. You have a lovely family, Mrs Burns." There was such a look of longing on her face when she said it, that their mother couldn't help asking, "And whit about your family, Morven? Rab said they passed away. Have you no other living relatives?"

Morven shook her head, giving the sleeping Isabella a peck on the cheek before she passed her back. "There's no one who cares for me now," she said sadly.

"That's no true!" Agnes piped up. "You saved my life, and that makes us almost kin, does it no, Ma?"

Mrs Burns chuckled. "Well, it makes us a deal more than neighbours, at any rate. Come round tomorrow night if you're free, lass. If you're no needed at the big house, then you're welcome to join us at supper."

"I'll be there," Morven smiled. "I've got to get back now, though. Factor McNab's still sick, and there's washing to be done." She hurried off, turning to wave at Agnes when she reached the end of the road, before disappearing round the corner.

The warm glow in Rab's stomach at the thought of seeing Morven at their house vanished as soon as he remembered what happened to the factor. Worries about witches and woven dolls, Cousin Betty and curses filled his head, and he climbed onto the cart with a heavy heart. He had an awful feeling that something bad was going to happen, but he had no idea yet what it might be.

When they got back home, the rest of the afternoon was spent helping his father threshing in the barn, separating the grain from the ears of corn and gathering the straw stalks left behind. It was back-breaking work, and even though Gil offered to lend a hand, Rab didn't want his younger brother shouldering such a weighty responsibility just yet.

By the time darkness fell, both Rab and his father were exhausted and eager for their supper. When they'd stowed their tools and stepped back into the house, they found the whole place in disarray. Agnes had clearly been milking her escape from the clutches of death for all it was worth, using her wounded knee as an excuse to shirk her chores. Gil had spent the day spreading lime on the fields, and his eyes were stinging so badly he could barely see to light the fire, never mind help get the supper ready. With their mother up to her arms in laundry, it was left to Nannie to see to the food. She wouldn't be seven for another few weeks, and hadn't yet mastered the art of making bannock bread that didn't taste like burnt leather.

"Agnes!" Rab rolled his eyes as soon as he saw her lolling by the fire instead of helping. "Get off your backside and help Nannie with the stew. It's your leg that's sore, no your hands. You can still peel a potato, can you no?" He hadn't forgotten the scare he'd got when he'd seen her lying in the path of the oncoming cart, so he tried to keep a smile on his lips and a touch of humour in his voice.

She wasn't amused, though. "Aye, I can peel well enough, but if you willnae help me by fetching in the tatties and the carrots from the kailyard, then how am I meant to manage with my leg all in pieces, hmm?" she grumbled.

Rab felt guilty when he saw their father look up from his books, ready to give her a telling off. "It's fine, Pa," he said, "she really did have a hard tumble today. I'll go and get the vegetables for the stew."

He hurried out to the kailyard behind the farmhouse to fill a bucket with potatoes and carrots, blowing on his fingers to keep the chill off as he pulled the roots from the hard earth. There was a sharp nip in the late-October air, and the waxing moon stared down at him as he worked, cold and unblinking in the night sky. There was no sign of storm clouds, or the sinister figures Rab had seen through the stone, but that didn't make him feel any less uneasy being out alone at night. He finished as fast as he could, lugging his full bucket back through the yard and washing the dirt from the vegetables at the hand pump.

He was about to return to the warmth of the kitchen, when something strange caught his eye.

Lying by the duck pond was a crumpled shape, its neck bent at an odd angle. Rab set his bucket down and went over to investigate. It was one of the ducks they reared for the winter season, their wings clipped while young to stop them flying south when the weather turned. The rest of the flock were huddled in their wooden pen, watching through the slats with frightened eyes.

Rab turned the duck over, looking for signs that a fox had got to it. There wasn't a mark on it. If it wasn't for its oddly twisted neck, Rab could've sworn there was nothing wrong with it. It was icy cold, though, and dead for some hours.

No matter how it had met its end, it meant Rab's family would be having meat tonight for the first time since he could remember, and he wasn't as sorry as he knew he should be for the mishap. He couldn't help feeling guilty for his eagerness when he showed his mother what he'd found, though, as her face fell, and he could see his father mentally re-calculating the flock's remaining value.

"Get a pot of water on to boil, Rab, and you can pluck it while Nannie makes the bannock. Aggie, will you get those tatties peeled? We'll put the duck on to roast instead of having a stew."

The younger children cheered, and Willie and John did a jig at the thought of having a taste of meat for the first time in ages. They couldn't afford to eat their own birds or cattle, but this duck wouldn't keep until the next time they went to market. Waste was something the Burns family could afford even less.

Rab tried not to wince at the heat scalding his hands as he plunged the duck into the bucket of boiling water and began stripping the feathers off, setting them aside so his mother could sell them to the mattress maker in town. He was ravenous by the time he was finished, and even the unpleasant business of gutting the bird with a sharp knife couldn't dull his appetite for roast meat. It was only when the knife jerked in his hand, hitting a hard object, that he realised there was something in the bird's stomach that shouldn't be there.

"Is that you done? About time, Rab. Your pa's belly's growling that loud they'll hear it halfway to Alloway by the time we get this supper done." His mother whisked the bird away to roast over the fire, and Rab was left staring down at the entrails on the carving board. He picked the knife back up and sliced open the stomach, searching for the object the duck had choked on. When he found it, he wished he hadn't gone looking.

Squeezed inside the small grey stomach was a large round stone with a circular hole in the middle. The very one he'd thrown away in the duck pond.

It had come back to haunt him.

Rab wasn't sure what made him lift the stone to his eye. Maybe it was the sight of Agnes sitting by the hearth with Isabella on her knee, with something curious clutched in her hands. It was half hidden in the folds of her dress, and she was showing it to the baby and jiggling it about to make Isabella giggle. Even in the dim light, Rab could see that it was woven out of straw.

He placed his eye to the hole and looked through it.

At once the house was plunged into darkness, save for the red glow of the kitchen fire. Dancing tongues of flame licked their way up the chimney, shining a spotlight on Agnes and the gurgling baby. On the wall next to his two sisters, shadows were forming, writhing like snakes just outside the circle of light. Black silhouettes were reaching out, grasping then recoiling, as though burned when they touched the warm glow surrounding Agnes and Isabella. Something was coming for his sisters, held back only by the invisible force that seemed to be protecting them. Rab opened his mouth to warn them, but just then, his mother called for him.

"Rab! Will you stop your dreaming and come and help me? John's got his finger stuck in the kettle spout again."

Rab dropped the stone, and it clattered onto the kitchen table. In an instant, the house was bathed in candlelight once more, and the menacing shadows disappeared. He took a long, shaky breath, then grabbed the stone. Stuffing it in his pocket, he promised himself that whatever dark magic it contained, he'd get rid of it that very night so it couldn't threaten his sisters ever again.

9

After supper, Rab couldn't find the stone.

It wasn't in his pocket, and no amount of hunting through the kitchen and parlour could help him locate it.

"Ach, Rab," his mother sleepily, "will you stop faffing about and go to bed? You're keeping the baby awake."

His father was already snoring, and the younger children were fast asleep in their trundle bed. Rab could barely keep his own eyes open, but the worry about what would happen when the last candle was snuffed— and the shadows closed in—made his heart race as he climbed to the loft.

Gil was sound asleep too, taking up most of the mattress and hogging the blanket. Rab rolled him over carefully to make enough room to lie down beside him. He didn't blow his candle out, though.

Tonight I'll keep watch, he vowed, peering at the shadows the candlelight sent flickering across the narrow loft steps. It almost looked as if they were creeping down to where Agnes and Isabella slept in the kitchen below.

If that stone causes any mischief tonight, I'll be ready. I'll... I'll...

Exhausted by the threshing work, his eyes began to close, and he drifted off into a deep, dreamless sleep.

He was awoken late the next morning by the sound of Agnes crying.

It took Rab a minute to work out where he was, and to remember what had happened the night before. When he did, he leapt up, following the sound of sobbing downstairs to the kitchen. Agnes was standing with an empty basket in her hand, tears running down her ashen face.

"Honest, Pa, I didnae break any!" she wailed. Their father was glaring at her with a face like thunder.

"Then explain to me how a whole coop of hens hasnae produced a single egg!" he growled. "If you've dropped the basket then just admit it. You know I dinnae tolerate lies, Aggie."

"I'm no lying!" Agnes cried even harder. "There's no eggs, and the best layers are looking sick and fevered. I've been feeding and watering them like I'm meant to, so I dinnae know whit's gone wrong."

Their father's frown grew deeper, and he strode out to the byre to investigate himself, leaving Agnes to crumple into a heap on a stool. Rab knew why she was so upset. The hens were her responsibility, and an important one at that. At nine years old, she was too young to work in the fields, and too small to be much help mucking out the byre or carrying heavy loads, so the job of keeping the hens fed, watered and clean fell to her alone. Aside from the milk, the eggs were the family's most dependable source of income.

If the large brood stopped laying, their family would be in trouble, and Agnes would shoulder the blame.

"Dinnae fret, Agnes," Rab tried to comfort her, putting his hand on her shoulder. "There was maybe a fox sniffing about last night and it's put them off laying. I'll set some traps round the byre and that'll sort it out, you'll see."

Agnes sniffed, tossing her head and shrugging his hand off. "Dinnae pretend you care, Rab," she muttered. "You're always looking for ways to get me in hot water with Pa, so I know you're right pleased about this."

"That's no true!" Rab protested.

"No? Who was it who told Pa I spilled the soup last week when he came in from the fields hungry for dinner?"

"It was a waste of good food! If you'd been paying attention and no playing games with Nannie it never would've—"

"And who told him I pinched the last of the apple pie that was being saved for Reverend Dalrymple visiting? Or spied on me having a wee nap when there was washing to be done? Or—"

"Och, Aggie!" Rab rolled his eyes. "I'm no trying to get you into trouble, but you're no a wee lassie anymore, and you need to be a bit more responsible."

As soon as the words were out of his mouth Rab regretted them. Agnes worked as hard as the rest of them, and if it wasn't for this cursed farm making them old before their time, she'd be allowed to be a little girl like she was supposed to, running in the fields with her friends instead of fretting over hens and slaving over tubs of washing. His sister's eyes filled with tears, and she turned away, stirring the porridge pot so fiercely Rab worried it might tumble into the fire.

Breakfast was a solemn affair. Their parents were worried about the hens, Agnes was worried about getting into trouble, and Rab was worried about finding the stone and keeping its sinister shadows at bay. The children could sense the sombre mood, and even John managed to eat his porridge in silence for once.

Only Gil seemed unconcerned, eating his burnt porridge with relish and grinning when he saw there were half-charcoaled bits of bannock left over from Nannie's efforts the night before. His enthusiasm made Rab smile. Nothing upset Gil for long, and nothing ever put him off his food. He was an island of cheerfulness in Mount Oliphant's sea of uncertainty, and Rab was glad the farm's hard work hadn't worn him down, the way it had with Rab and Agnes.

He watched his sister spooning porridge into their siblings' bowls, helping Willie spread butter on his bread and wiping the dribbled oats from John's chin. Her face was tired and pinched; she looked exhausted. *If I kept as close an eye out for her as I do for Gil, she wouldnae have so many cares weighing her down,* Rab thought, remembering all the times he'd shouldered extra work so that Gil could take a lighter share. When was the last time he'd done anything for Agnes?

"Are you coming, Rab?" his father asked suddenly. Rab looked up to see him already at the door, and Gil pulling his boots on.

"Whit? Oh... I..."

"Dreaming again?" his father frowned. "The barn needs work on the back wall afore the storms come. By the looks of it, we'll be in for a windy end to autumn, with rains and thunder to come, so we need to shore up the cracks to secure the harvest."

"Right, Pa, I'll be there in a wee minute."

The hunt for the strange stone would have to wait. As usual, there was work to be done first.

The rest of the day was spent fixing the broken-down barn wall. Rab wasn't sure their efforts would be enough to protect the precious harvest inside from the coming winter storms, but it was the best they could do. They couldn't afford a mason to do the job properly. Hoisting heavy stones and sealing the cracks with mortar was tiring work, but at least it kept his mind from the odd things he'd seen over the last week.

When the night had closed in and they'd finally finished their work, the sight Rab saw in the yard made his skin crawl.

There was a hunched figure standing by the water pump, loose ends of a black shawl fluttering in the moonlight. It looked as though the figure had stepped right out of the missing stone, the dark shadows from the night before condensing into a living form. Then the figure turned to look their way, and Rab recognised the wrinkled face hidden beneath the shawl.

"Cousin Betty!" Gil grinned at the old woman. "I didnae know you were coming tonight. Is your arm better?"

"It'll be fine, Gil. It's no as bad as it was."

The way she cradled her wrist close to her chest like a wounded animal made Rab seriously doubt her words.

"Come away in then, Betty," William Burns said. "It's too cold a night for someone your age to be gadding about the countryside." Their father wasn't much more pleased to see Betty than Rab was. He wasn't keen on the old woman. He thought she gossiped too much and filled his children's heads with superstitious nonsense, but he was too polite to make her feel unwelcome.

"Cousin Betty! Whit are you doing here with your arm still in such a state?" Rab's mother asked when they stepped into the kitchen. "Should you no be resting at the cottage?"

"Ach, I'm no use to anyone there," Betty muttered. "You need all the help you can get with the wee ones here."

Despite the fright she'd given him, Rab was glad she was here where he could keep an eye on her. *Who knows whit mischief she's been getting up to in the cottage with her weaving and her witchcraft?* he thought darkly.

A loud knock on the door made him jump. Forgetting all about her sore leg, Agnes ran to answer it, throwing her arms round the young woman on the doorstep.

"Morven! You came!"

"I'm glad you could make it, lass," Mrs Burns beamed. "I was hoping they wouldnae keep you back at the big house."

Cousin Betty scowled when she saw who the visitor was. If Rab didn't know better, he might've thought the old woman was jealous of the maid getting the warm welcome she'd been denied.

"I would've thought a wee hussy like you would have too many admirers to visit to bother with the likes of *my* family," Betty muttered, putting her good arm round Nannie's shoulder. The little girl shrugged it off and ran up to Morven instead.

"Did you *really* jump in front of a team of horses to save our Aggie from getting trampled yesterday?" she gasped. "Come and tell us all about it!"

The children crowded round her, pulling her to the hearth to hear her story, leaving Betty standing awkwardly on her own.

"Gil, set the table, will you?" their father said. "The supper's nearly done."

"I can—" Betty began.

"Dinnae worry about it, Cousin Betty." Gil jumped up to help. "You rest that arm of yours."

"Rab, can you fetch me another bucket of water?" their mother asked.

"I'm no an invalid, I can—"

"The bucket's too heavy, Cousin Betty. I'll get it." Rab hurried out to the pump, unwilling to leave his family alone with her for any longer than he had to. Only a short time ago the old woman had been a welcome visitor, and the thought of listening to her tales of magic and mystery round the hearth had made many a working day go faster for him. Now she made him nervous, and the sight of her anywhere near Agnes and the baby made the hair on the back of his neck prickle uncomfortably.

It was Morven who was given the place of honour at the supper table, and Morven whose stories the children were eager to hear as they ate.

"Whit's it like working at the big house?" Agnes wanted to know. "Is it true the family eat all their meals off silver plates?"

"Do they stuff themselves with cake and puddings all day long?" Willie put in, his eyes filled with longing.

"Never mind that, are the rumours true that Factor McNab's fading fast and willnae last the week?" Gil asked. The whole table was silent for a moment, every face turning to Morven.

The maid looked sad, and she nodded. "It seems likely. Doctor Campbell doesnae hold out much hope for him."

Rab could see his father fighting hard to keep the relief out of his eyes, and his mother looking guilty, as though her thoughts were not as sympathetic as she wanted them to be.

Cousin Betty's face grew even more sour as she glared at Morven. "It's witchcraft that's at the bottom of this," she warned. "Halloween's coming and there's mischief brewing."

Rab felt such a jolt of surprise at her words he nearly fell off his chair. *Is she actually admitting it?* he wondered.

"Ach, Betty," his mother sighed, "you see the supernatural everywhere. The factor choked on his beef and had a heart attack trying to cough it back up. Whit's that got to do with your fairy tales?"

"They're no just stories," Betty insisted. "Witches are real. And if you dinnae take me seriously, you'll regret it!"

Rab shuddered. It sounded like a threat.

"Angus McNab was enchanted, I know that for a fact. The witches are gathering for Halloween, and they're looking for—"

"That's enough!" A fist thumped down on the table, making them all jump. It wasn't William Burns who had interrupted Betty, though, it was Morven.

Her eyes were flashing, and in the candlelight Rab couldn't tell whether she was angry or upset. "Those are *wicked* words, Betty Davidson. Wicked!" she cried, her voice shaking. "A Christian woman shouldnae say such things, especially around wee ones who dinnae know better than to believe them."

"Hear, hear," Rab's father echoed, standing up to put an end to the meal. "We'll have no more of your old wives' tales, Betty. I've had enough of you filling my children's heads with nonsense for one night."

"Well, I'll hold my tongue and help in other ways then, shall I?" Betty muttered, stacking the dirty pots in a bucket with her good hand.

"I'll get those." Morven cleared the rest of the dishes and followed Betty over to the dresser to fetch a cloth. A few seconds later, there came an almighty crash and a yelp of surprise.

"Betty!" they heard Morven cry, "I told you to watch you didnae knock that jug over! Now look whit you've done!"

Rab looked round to see Cousin Betty standing pale-faced over a shattered jug, the precious buttermilk it had contained pooling on the floor.

"Och, Betty!" Mrs Burns wailed. "Whit have you gone and done? I was saving that to exchange with Peggy Roberts for the sewing thread I'm in sore need of."

"It wasnae me! I didnae—"

"I think it's time you went home, Betty," William Burns sighed. "That arm of yours is clearly no up to housework yet. Come with me and I'll get the cart out. I'll no have you walking home on such a cold night."

With that, Betty was dismissed. Rab wasn't sorry to see the back of the old woman, but there was still a small part of him that felt bad for her when his brothers and sisters turned away without saying goodbye and steered Morven to the best spot by the fire. The nasty look Betty threw Morven as she left made Rab's blood run cold. If the maid wasn't careful, she could end up being cursed just like Factor McNab.

Rab wasn't sure how many more things he could worry about without his head exploding.

When he'd finished helping his mother wash up, Rab joined the others sitting round the kitchen fire with Morven. The maid was sewing Agnes's initials into the handkerchief she'd given her, and his sister was watching the needle fly in her deft fingers with awe. When she'd finished, she put the pretty piece of linen in Agnes's pocket for safe keeping and took Isabella to rock her to sleep. It was a cosy scene, and Rab felt a twinge of envy when he saw Agnes curl up next to Morven, the baby gurgling happily in the maid's arms. It was as though she'd taken his place as the eldest. Then he remembered that Morven had lost her own family, and he felt ashamed at the thought.

Morven looked up at him, smiling in her cat-like way, and shifted to make room for him on the bench. Rab sat down eagerly. *Am I jealous because the wee ones are giving Morven all their attention instead of me, or because I want to keep Morven's attention all to myself?* he wondered. Either way, he was glad she'd included him.

"Go on with whit you were saying, Morven," Agnes urged, scowling at Rab for interrupting the story. "Why do you no like Cousin Betty to talk of witches?"

With their father away taking Betty home, and their mother busy sweeping the parlour, the subject was a safe one to bring up again.

"Because folk say it was witches that caused my family's fever," Morven said, her eyes growing sad in the firelight. "It happened some years back, right afore Halloween, and gossips like Betty Davidson said I was the root of the trouble. They drove me out of my village with little more than the clothes I had on my back. I lost everything—my family, my friends, and even my dignity, just because some wicked old maids couldnae tell the difference between medical troubles and superstition!"

"Is it because you made up poultices for them?" Rab asked, "like the one you brought to Cousin Betty?"

"Aye, that and..." Morven trailed off, giving Rab a small shake of her head and looking away quickly. She was warning him not to ask any more questions.

Not here, she was saying. *Not now.*

Then she forced a smile and said brightly, "Who wants to hear a song? Agnes? I bet you've got a pretty voice to match your pretty face, will you join me?" She began to sing the children's favourite ballad, and they joined in eagerly with the chorus of 'Dumbarton's Drums', their faces glowing with delight in the firelight as they clapped along.

Rab sat in silence, staring into the fire and wondering how he could have been such a fool. He'd got it all wrong. He'd thought Cousin Betty was the one who'd be able to tell him what the woven figure in the church and the disturbing sights he'd been seeing in the stone meant. He'd thought she was the expert on the signs of witchcraft and the ways to spot dark magic.

Now he knew Morven was the one he needed to turn to for advice.

10

Rab didn't get a chance to speak to Morven before she left.

He wished he had. The next morning, something so bad happened it was clear the farm was cursed.

Rab woke to the sound of Agnes crying again, but this time their father wasn't shouting. When Rab went downstairs he found him pacing about the parlour, exchanging hushed words with their mother.

"Whit's going on?" he asked, looking at Agnes. It was then that he noticed she was holding an empty bucket and milk jug, and he realised what had happened even before his mother told him.

"The milk's dried up," she sighed, wringing her hands. "The cows' udders are all shrivelled like prunes, and Agnes couldnae get a single drop from any of them this morning."

The hens weren't laying and the cows weren't producing. No eggs and no milk—the two jobs that Agnes was often left in charge of while their mother fed the baby. Rab was starting to wonder if it wasn't his sister who was cursed rather than the farm.

"Are they sick like the hens?" he wondered. "Do you think—"

"I dinnae know, Rab," his father growled. His temper was frayed, and it wasn't just the sick animals that had vexed him. Isabella had been crying all night, and no amount of pacing up and down by either his mother or Agnes had been able to coax her back to sleep. They were all tired and worn ragged round the edges this morning.

"Instead of standing there with your mouth open, I need you to run down to Alloway and find Sandy Harris. Fetch him up here—he might know whit to do."

Sandy was one of his father's best friends from their Alloway days, and had often given him advice when William Burns first set up a farm. If anyone knew what to do about the sick animals, it was Sandy.

Rab pulled on one of his boots and tried to gulp down a slice of buttered toast at the same time, but half asleep, he managed to drop most of it into Isabella's cradle as he stumbled round the parlour looking for the other boot.

"Och, Rab! Watch whit you're doing," his mother warned. "No wonder the wee thing's still howling if you're using her bed as a midden!"

"Sorry, Bella." Rab leaned down to retrieve his toast and give the crying baby a kiss on the cheek. It wasn't only the bread he found down the side of her cradle, though. His fingers brushed something hard, and he pulled it out. Isabella had been lying on a polished stone with a circular hole in the middle.

That's where it disappeared to! Rab gasped to himself. *No wonder the baby's been screaming her head off half the night with that infernal thing poking into her back.*

Almost as soon as he removed it, Isabella stopped crying and settled down to sleep.

"Would you look at that!" Their mother rolled her eyes. "If I'd known all I had to do to get her to settle was dump a loaf of bread over her, we'd all have slept soundly last night."

Rab pretended to smile, but his heart was thumping so loud he was afraid his mother would hear it. He'd found the stone that was full of shadows and secrets— now he had to get rid of it before the darkness leaked out and threatened his family.

"I'll be back as soon as I can!" he called, closing the door behind him. He knew fetching Sandy Harris was an important job, but he had an even more urgent one to do first.

This time, when he ran down the lane to Alloway, he didn't look back. He didn't want to see if a sinister figure dressed in black was following him behind the hedgerows, and he certainly didn't want to look through the stone ever again.

I dinnae know where this thing came from, or why it's latched onto me like a leech, but I know where it's going.

He headed for the one place he felt sure the darkness in the stone wouldn't be able to escape from: the hallowed ground of the old kirk.

It was still early morning, and the mist from the River Doon shrouded the churchyard in wispy white tendrils, cold and insubstantial as the fingers of a ghost. Just for a moment, Rab thought he saw a flicker of firelight coming from the far end of the kirkyard.

He went to investigate, stepping carefully over the crumbled remains of gravestones until he came to the small building at the back. It was about the size of a large hen house, but much grander, with stone pillars on either side of the entrance gates and grinning gargoyles set round the sloped roof.

Rab remembered his father telling him that someone very important was buried in the old mausoleum, but he couldn't remember who it was. There was nothing carved above the entrance, no name or date, but the heavy padlock chained to the rusty gates made it clear that visitors and their questions were not welcome.

Rab thought he caught sight of the flickering red light again, coming from inside the stone tomb. He leaned against the bars, staring into the burial chamber's black depths. He couldn't see inside; it was too dark.

It must've been the sun peeping through the mist and flashing off the gates, he thought, not entirely convinced by the explanation.

But he didn't have time to worry about it now.

Rab shivered and looked around for a suitable place to bury the stone. He didn't want to disturb any of the graves that sat sombre and silent in the tangled undergrowth, so he headed for the yew tree that grew near the entrance of the crumbling kirk. Cousin Betty had told him one night that the sacred trees were grown in churchyards to prevent the rising of ghosts and apparitions, their roots holding the dead firmly underground. If anything could keep the evil in the stone from returning to haunt him, it was the ancient yew.

He rounded the corner of the wall and stopped dead.

Something was moving inside the old kirk.

Rab stumbled back, ducking down behind the statue of a weeping angel that guarded the ruins of a headstone. He peered through the gloom, his eyes narrowing when he saw that the woven image of the Devil was still standing on the threshold of the church, the straw dog's muzzle facing him menacingly.

Maybe it's a tool for summoning, he thought, his mind racing. *And maybe it's already done its wicked work.*

Every hair on the back of his neck prickled, urging him to run, but he gritted his teeth and crept forward, hiding behind the thick trunk of the yew tree. He had to get to the bottom of this. He had to find out what all the frightening omens meant and where they were coming from. Most of all, he had to find out how to stop them.

When he gazed into the dark belly of the abandoned kirk, one of his questions was answered. He now knew for certain where the dark signs were coming from. But that only deepened the mystery of *why*.

A familiar figure was hobbling round the crumbling walls, her eerie chants echoing in the broken rafters. Rab couldn't make out Cousin Betty's words, but they weren't in any language he'd ever heard. Through the thick screen of ivy and weeds, he could see her placing more straw dolls on the empty windowsills where glass had once been. The figures were ugly and misshapen, their heads too big for their bodies and their arms and legs long and spindly. Rab was sure they were demons, witches, and all manner of unnatural creatures.

Why is she doing this? he wondered. He wished he had the courage to confront the old woman he'd once thought of as a friend. She wasn't simply his mother's cousin; she was the closest thing he had to a grandmother now that the previous generation had all passed away. He couldn't understand why she was responsible for this wickedness.

If she's summoning Old Nick and his witches for Halloween, then I have to stop her! Rab thought desperately, trying to force his feet to move. But as the old woman came creeping out of the church, the edges of her black shawl flapping raggedly in the breeze, he ducked back, too afraid to show himself.

Cousin Betty was too powerful a witch for him to

stop on his own. He needed help.

I cannae tell my parents, he thought. *Pa would clip me round the ear for talking nonsense, and Ma wouldnae believe Cousin Betty was capable of dark magic for a second.*

Gil was his closest companion, but he didn't want his younger brother mixed up in this if he could help it. It was bad enough that the shadows in the stone had gathered round Agnes and the baby, its magic sickening the chickens and the cows and threatening their farm. There was only one person left who had hinted at knowing more about witches than she let on, and that was Morven.

She's been accused of witchcraft afore, she said as much last night, Rab thought. *It'll maybe dredge up some painful memories talking about it, but she might know some of the ways the villagers warded against the dark magic they thought she possessed.*

Morven was his last hope to solve the mystery before Halloween, and he was certain she'd help him. He'd never met anyone who'd suffered so much loss and hardship but was still so kind.

I'll talk to her tonight when she comes over, he decided. *We'll put a stop to Cousin Betty's wickedness together.*

First, he had to get rid of the cursed object that was causing him and his family so much grief. He pulled the stone from his pocket, shuddering at its cold weight in his palm. It seemed as though he held a fragment chipped from the very wall dividing earth and hell, and through the tiny spyhole he could catch glimpses of that demonic world.

"Back to the depths where you belong," he muttered, digging a deep hole under the yew tree's roots with a broken branch. "Stay there and rot, and dinnae come chasing after me and my family anymore."

He hurled the stone to the bottom of the hole, covering it up with earth and patting it down firmly. There would be no more sightings of witches or shadows through its hole, and no more sick animals on the farm. His family was safe.

For now, Rab thought ominously, glancing back at the woven figures leering out at him from the kirk windows.

As he stood up and brushed the dirt from his breeches, a loud cry shook the air. Something passed so close to his face he could feel the beating of wings and the sharp talons that raked his hair, missing his eyes by inches. Before he could catch a glimpse of the creature through the mist, it was gone, leaving him shaken and breathless.

Maybe the old yew isnae as good at holding the spirits down as I thought, he shuddered, turning tail and heading for the safety of the lane.

He knew it was only a bird, disturbed by his digging around the tree roots, but after all the strange things he'd been seeing, his mind was playing tricks on him.

Rab hesitated at the crossroads. His heart was telling him to run straight to Doonholm to speak with Morven, but his head was telling him to follow his father's instructions and fetch Sandy Harris.

I'll see Morven soon enough, he reminded himself. *Right now there's a barn full of sick cows and a brood of hens to be seen to.*

Despite his misgivings, duty came first, and he broke into a run, heading for the farmer's cottage on the outskirts of Alloway.

11

"So, you think the stone was cursed?" Rab whispered, glancing across the yard to make sure the farmhouse door was firmly shut and no one could hear them. "You think I was right to get rid of it?"

"Aye, Rab," Morven nodded, pumping more water into the bucket to wash the rest of the supper dishes. "Those things are called 'hag stones', and if you go carrying one around then witches can sniff you out and cause all manner of mischief."

"Like stopping hens from laying and cows from making milk?"

"Things of that nature, I suppose."

Morven didn't sound as sure about it as Rab hoped. With his family's eyes on him all evening, he hadn't been able to tell her the full story of what he'd seen over the last week. Agnes had demanded every second of Morven's attention, and Gil made jokes that Rab was sweet on the maid any time he tried to get a moment alone with her. Before he could tell her about Cousin Betty's woven dolls, she surprised him by asking, "Is that all there is to it? A stone you saw witches and shadows through? You havenae seen anything else?"

"Like whit?" Rab said, wondering how much she already knew.

"Well..." Morven's eyes narrowed in the darkness, and she hesitated before telling him, "I've seen unnatural things happen afore, when my family passed. Things that other folk wouldnae believe if I told them."

Rab's heart beat faster. He hadn't wanted to push her into telling him how her family died for fear of upsetting her, but he knew her story might hold the key to unlocking the mystery of Cousin Betty's straw dolls. "I'd believe anything you told me, Morven, you know that," he said, giving her a reassuring smile.

She smiled back, giving his hand a soapy squeeze as a thankyou. "Well then, I'll tell you whit happened to my family, if you promise to keep it to yourself. I dinnae want other folks gossiping about me the way they did back in my old village."

Rab nodded eagerly, and she went on, "It was five years ago now, in the run-up to Halloween. I got into a quarrel with one of the local busy-bodies, a spinster by the name of Jessie McGuire. She was an uncanny-looking old soul and no mistake, with her white hair flying about and her tartan shawl that hadnae been washed in fifty years. Nobody liked Jessie—she was always meddling in other folk's affairs, but if I'd known she was a witch, I would've stayed well clear of her."

"A witch?" Rab gasped. "How did you find out?"

"No long after the quarrel, Ma got sick—real sick. Then Pa sickened, and one by one the wee ones got the fever and all. Jessie was punishing me for my sharp tongue, and there wasnae a thing I could do about it."

"But how did you know it was her, and no just bad luck?"

Morven's voice grew even softer, and Rab had to strain to hear her over the whistling of the wind round the barns. "Because I saw her through her window the night after the quarrel. I'd gone to her cottage to apologise, but after I saw whit she was making, I ran off with my heart half-stopped in fright."

"Whit did you see?" Rab urged, dropping all pretence of washing the dishes and leaning closer. "Whit was it?"

"It was dolls," Morven whispered back. "Little dolls all made from straw. That might sound innocent enough, but they looked so like my family I knew there was mischief being woven into them."

Rab's eyes widened until they were dark circles of fear in the moonlight. He was right. Cousin Betty and her dolls were behind all of the misfortunes that had befallen the farm. "But how do you know they gave your family the fever?" he asked. "Did you hear her chanting things, or cursing them, or—"

"Aye, she was chanting strange words over them that

night, that's for sure," Morven said gravely. "But that's no how I knew they caused my family's fever. They sickened and died on All Hallow's Eve, and there was nothing I could do to bring down their fever. Some local women came the next day to help me wash and dress the bodies in their best clothes for burial—that's when we found them."

"Found whit?" Rab's voice was barely above a whisper now.

"The *dolls.*" Morven's voice cracked, and she half choked on the memory. "My ma and pa, my brothers and sisters—they all had one of those wee dolls in their pocket. That was when the villagers started pointing their fingers at me, calling me a witch, and forcing me to pack up and leave. As if I'd hurt my own family! As if I'd do such a thing to my poor wee Peggy—" Morven's voice finally broke, and she hid her face in her hands.

Rab shifted awkwardly from foot to foot, unsure how best to comfort her. She wasn't his sister, so he couldn't give her a hug, but standing there staring at her crying wasn't much use either. He settled for putting his hand on her shoulder and giving it a squeeze, and she patted it gratefully.

"So how come when Cousin Betty talked of witches gathering afore Halloween the other night, you got angry? How come you said your family died of medical troubles? Would it no be better to tell the truth?"

Morven eyes flashed through her tears, and for a moment her white teeth looked like fangs again. "Have you no been listening to a word I've been saying? I've already been driven from my home because folks talked of witchcraft and laid the blame for it on me. The last thing I want is an old gossip like Betty Davidson hearing my story and spreading it about Alloway that I'm an accused witch. Besides, I know your pa doesnae like anyone talking of superstitious things, and your ma might think I'm a bad influence on the wee ones, and no ask me round anymore."

"You like my family, then?" Rab couldn't help asking.

"Aye, Rab, that I do," Morven nodded. "I've no felt this welcome anywhere in a long time. You're lucky to have them."

Rab felt the knot of fear in his stomach tighten. "If everything you said is true, then I'm maybe no as lucky as you think. I may no have them for much longer."

"Whit do you mean?" Morven frowned. "I thought you said you'd buried the stone and that was the end of Betty Davidson's mischief?"

"That stone was just the beginning. She's been making dolls, Morven, like the ones you described. I've seen her with my own eyes. There's one for each of my family, even wee Isabella."

Morven gasped in horror. "She's threatening the baby? Rab! We have to stop her!"

"I know! But I dinnae know how to get hold of... Hey! Wait a wee minute!"

"Whit?"

"I know where two of the dolls are!" Rab thought back to the day he'd visited Betty's cottage with Agnes, and how he'd seen their cousin slip something to his sister when they were leaving. "I think Agnes has two of the dolls—one for her and Isabella. I've seen her playing with something in the evenings, but she willnae let me near enough to show me whit it is."

"Then they're both in mortal danger," Morven told him. "That'll be why Agnes near got killed by that cart on market day, and why her luck with the chickens and the cows has soured so badly. We can only thank heavens the baby hasnae been affected yet."

"But I thought the stone—"

"Forget the hag stone!" Morven snapped. "That's dead and buried. The magic's in the dolls, and we have to get rid of them, Rab, or whit happened to my family will happen to yours."

"But why?" Rab cried. "Why would Betty do such a wicked thing? There's no love lost between her and Pa, but she's been Ma's right hand for years now, and treated me and the wee ones like we were her own."

"Witches crave power more than anything. The lust for it turns their love to hate, and makes them blind to anything that stands in their way. If Betty's meeting with her coven at Halloween, and she brings them the gift of your family's souls, it'll make her the most powerful witch of the lot."

"Coven?" Rab blinked, bewildered. "Whit's that?"

"Her group of witches, the ones she's tied to by ancient magic. Those ties are thicker than the bonds between kin. Betty'll do anything to please her master and gain more power, and a baby to bring up as a witch from the cradle is whit he craves the most."

"Betty's master?" Rab gasped. "You dinnae mean—"

"RAB!" Agnes called from the doorway. "Are you going to stand there gabbing all night? The wee ones want to hear some more of Morven's songs afore bed and you're hogging her all to yourself. She's no your sweetheart, you know. She's got admirers all the way from here to Auchenshuggle, and you're a deal too young and stupid for the likes of her."

"Ach, away and boil your head in the stew pot, Agnes," Rab yelled back. "Morven's been helping me wash the dishes, is all." He'd vowed to be nicer to his sister since he'd seen the shadows menacing her, but she'd made him blush in front of Morven, and that was about the worst crime she could commit.

Morven merely smiled her cat-like smile and waved Agnes over. "Come out here a wee minute, pet. I want to ask you something."

Agnes stuck her feet into her mother's clogs and came

clomping into the yard. "Whit's up? Has my daft brother been boring you to death with those silly poems of his?"

Rab opened his mouth to protest, but Morven held up a hand to silence him. She pointed at the small bulge in his sister's pinafore pocket, reminding him they had far more important matters to attend to than his wounded pride. "Whit have you got in there, pet?" Morven asked softly. "Is it a dolly?"

A guilty look flashed across Agnes's face, and she turned on Rab angrily. "Have you been spying on me, Rab Burns? Cause if you have, I'll—"

"You're no in any trouble, my pretty wee lassie," Morven soothed. "I just wondered whit you've been carrying around. Will you show me?"

Agnes hesitated, sticking her hand in her pocket and holding on tightly to the secret it contained. "Cousin Betty said I wasnae to show anyone," she said, torn between wanting to please Morven and not wanting to betray her cousin's trust.

"I'll tell you why I want to know, then you can decide if you want to show me, how about that?" Morven smiled. "Well, some years back, my wee Peggy was given a doll by one of the farmer's wives. It was made of straw, and it was the spitting image of her, right down to her pretty hair. She played with it all the time, and even kept it on her pillow at night. Only, she didn't know that giant ticks nest in straw, and one morning she woke up covered all over in spots and boils from their bites that made her face swell up and—"

"You think there's ticks in these dolls?" Agnes whipped the two small figures from her pocket before Morven could finish her invented story. In the moon's pale glow, Rab could see the images of Agnes and the baby that Cousin Betty had been making in the yard the day he passed by on Meg.

Morven nodded gravely. "I'm afraid so, pet. I can see their wee legs wriggling about and their hungry jaws ready to bite. They'll need to be burned if you're to avoid being covered in spots and boils like Peggy."

"Then you take them!" Agnes thrust the dolls at Morven, as eager to be rid of them now as she'd been to hold onto them a moment ago.

Morven leapt back as though Agnes was giving her a bunch of stinging nettles.

She's being a wee bit dramatic, Rab thought. *She's already talked Agnes into handing them over.* "Here, I'll take them," he said, snatching the dolls and putting them in his own pocket before Agnes could protest. Her bottom lip trembled when she saw them disappear, but Morven was quick to give her a hug.

"Dinnae fret, pet. I'll make you a new doll, a proper stuffed one with a cloth face and a fancy dress—would you like that?"

Agnes nodded eagerly. With the farm eating up all

the money, their parents couldn't afford much in the way of toys for the children. They had to make do with hoops from old cart wheels and wonky spinning tops that never stayed upright long no matter how hard they were whipped.

"Then let's go and sing those songs. I've been dying to hear your sweet wee voice again—you sound like the nightingale in the story I told you about last night."

Agnes beamed with pleasure, taking Morven's hand and skipping with her into the house. Rab didn't follow them in. Instead, he fetched a spare tinderbox from the tool rack, taking it behind the barn and setting the two small figures down against the wall where they were sheltered from draughts. After a few strikes of the flint, a spark set the straw ablaze, and Rab watched in relief as the images of Agnes and Isabella burned away to glowing cinders.

That's another problem solved, he thought, kicking the blackened heap and scattering the ashes. *Now all I have to worry about is how to stop whitever dark spells Cousin Betty will try to weave next.*

12

Next day, the farm was back to normal.

Rab woke to the sound of his mother humming happily as she counted the egg collection, and Agnes clattering about with pails full of milk. His father was already out in the barn sorting threshed straw into bundles for thatching, and Rab spent his first relaxed breakfast in ages having a fork fight with Gil to see who could spear the most bannock.

"Hey, you big thief! That was my piece!" Gil cried as Rab whipped another bit of buttered bread away before he could stick it in his mouth.

"Too slow! You have to be quick if you want to... Cheat! You cannae use a knife too!"

"Tell that to William Wallace! He didnae win his wars with only a fork!"

"That's as maybe, but I'll win this one with just my two hands!" Rab grabbed his brother in a headlock and tickled him till Gil was begging for mercy. The boys were still laughing when their father put his head round the door and called them out to work.

Rab put his boots on with more enthusiasm than he'd felt in a long while. There might still be trouble coming before Halloween, but now that he had Morven as an ally, he felt sure he could keep his family safe from Cousin Betty. His parents put the recovery of the hens and cows down to the suggestion Sandy Harris had made about their feed, so no one suspected there was any more to it than that. Rab had been so worried, he'd nearly told his secrets to Gil. He was glad he could spare his younger brother a share of the weight he'd been carrying for the past week.

"Hey, look, Rab! You can see all the way to America from here," Gil grinned as they balanced on the farmhouse roof, trying to clean the worst of the soot from the chimney with a long brush. The kitchen fire had been playing up, and the cooking smoke the night before had been black, even though Anes hadn't burnt the bannock bread for once.

"You're soft in the head, Gil. That's clouds on the horizon you're looking at. And anyway, do you no think you'd see Ireland first afore you saw the New World?" Rab laughed, shaking his head at his brother's made-up geography.

"Aye, but imagine you *could* see America from here, and travel to it as easy as getting to Dublin. We could bring back sugar and cotton and all sorts of things for market, instead of boring old eggs and butter. When I'm older I'm going to sail there, and build a farm in Virginia, and—"

"Ach, Gil! If you're no careful you willnae grow up at all," Rab yelped, grabbing his brother before he leaned too far over the roof to watch a flock of wild geese flying south. "You'll be broken to bits by a fall and buried in the kirkyard with a big stone saying, *'Here lies the daftest wee gowk that ever lived.'* Pay attention, will you? That's a nasty drop, and the wind's picking up."

The day had started fine and clear, but now there were dark clouds rolling in from the east, heavy with rain and threatening thunder. The boys finished up quickly, clambering down the ladder and running for shelter just as the first large drops began to fall. Within moments, the rain was pounding off the farmhouse roof, driven so hard by the oncoming storm that Rab could almost feel the walls shaking.

"That's the end of outside work for today then," he sighed. "I reckon it's back to threshing for me and mucking out the byre for you. See you at supper."

He was pulling his jacket over his head to make a dash for the barn when Gil called, "Could we no swap? I can take a turn of the threshing for once, Rab; I'm nearly as old as you."

You've just turned eleven, Rab thought sadly. *And even if you were my age, I'd no want your arms to ache so much at the end of the day you'd thank the surgeon if he took them off for you.* He didn't say that out loud, though. He grinned instead and called over his shoulder, "Whit, and spend all afternoon up to my knees in cow muck? No thanks, Gil. I'm the biggest, so I get to shirk in the barn and leave all the hardest jobs for you."

He didn't look back to see if his brother believed him or not.

The threshing work was every bit as bad as he expected, and by suppertime his shoulders were so sore from swinging the flail he could barely lift his spoon. Now that her secret stash of dolls had been discovered and burned, Agnes had no reason to avoid the chair next to him, and she managed to sneak more food from his plate than he'd ever have allowed Nannie. For once he didn't begrudge it. He was just glad the threat to her and the baby had been prevented by Morven's quick thinking.

He was too tired to even grumble at Gil for taking up more than his fair share of the mattress as they tumbled into bed in the loft, and he fell asleep as soon as his head hit the lumpy pillow. There were no more nightmares of witches or dark shadows. His dreams were full of images of a golden autumn sun streaming through the leaves of an apple tree, the smell of fresh-baked bramble pie drifting on the breeze, and a glimpse of a pair of beautiful cat-green eyes behind a scullery window.

Suddenly the window opened with a bang, and Rab

jerked awake, hitting his head on the low rafters.

It wasn't the one in his dream that had opened. There was a small window set into the loft wall, and the shutters had been blown open, letting the full force of the gale in. Rab clambered over his sleeping brother, careful not to wake him even though he knew it would take several tonnes of dynamite to rouse Gil when he was snoring so loud. One shutter had been pulled half off its hinges, and Rab looked out into the night as he struggled to fix it.

The rain had stopped, the wet ground shimmering like a carpet of jewels in the moonlight. The trees were tossing wildly in the wind, their branches groaning as though in pain. A sharp nip was in the air, and there was something eerie about the way the darkness seeped like ink across the fields, blotting out the familiar landscape and shrouding it in mystery.

Rab shivered, redoubling his efforts to close the shutters. He'd just got the squint one straightened, when something came swooping out of the night, flying right at him. He stumbled back in fright, tripping over the edge of the mattress and landing with a thump on the floorboards. There was a loud screeching sound, a ghostly flapping of white around his head, and then silence.

Rab had squeezed his eyes shut in fright, and now he opened them slowly, dreading what he might see. Two great orbs were staring back at him, so close he could see his face reflected in them. For one awful moment he thought some terrible demon had come to claim him.

Wait, that's no a monster...

Rab sighed in relief. He was staring into the eyes of a giant owl. The bird tilted its head at a quizzical angle, hooted softly, and dropped what it was holding in one of its talons. The object rolled across the windowsill and landed at Rab's feet. The owl hooted once more, then took off, disappearing into the night.

Rab stretched out a trembling hand and grasped the object the owl had left. It was covered in a layer of dirt, but even before he cleaned it on the edge of his nightshirt, Rab knew what he was holding.

It was the hag stone he'd hidden in the kirkyard.

But I buried it under the yew tree! Is this Cousin Betty's doing? he wondered, his heart pounding. *Is she going to curse our farm and our family? Is the milk going to dry up again, and are the shadows going to come creeping back for the wee ones?*

The stone was so cold he could feel it burning his palm. He drew his arm back angrily, ready to toss the cursed thing out into the night.

Then he stopped.

Something was moving in the lane leading from their yard. Rab could just make out a small figure in the dark, walking slowly towards the fields as though half asleep. It didn't take him more than an instant to recognise his sister's familiar outline. *Agnes!* She was carrying a blanket in her arms, and Rab knew exactly what the bundle contained.

He was about to run down to fetch her in, when the hag stone shivered in his hand, growing so cold he could hardly bear to hold onto it. It wanted him to do something—something he feared more than anything else. He battled with it, his own desire to drop it from the window fighting against the stone's command to raise it to his eye.

The stone won.

With shaking fingers, Rab lifted it and looked through its round hole.

The sky blazed with lightning, the racing clouds split apart by sparks of fire that arced to the ground. The storm-tossed trees were not groaning now but screaming, their cries echoing above the howling of the wind. At the far end of the lane, black shapes circled Agnes, unnaturally long fingers twitching out from ragged cloaks to stroke the sleeping-walking girl, urging her to follow them.

Before Rab even knew what he was doing, he'd shoved the stone in his pocket, stumbled down the loft ladder, and pulled on his boots and jacket. He hesitated at the door, then grabbed the storm lantern that hung on the wall for emergencies, wasting precious seconds lighting the candle inside. The flame wasn't very bright, but the smoky glass would at least protect it from being blown out.

Maybe I should wake Pa? he thought, glancing round at the sleeping figures in the wall bed. *Maybe he's the one who should be dealing with this?*

There was no time. He'd never be able to make his father understand his tangled tale of witches leading Agnes into the night before she was long gone with her precious bundle. It was up to him to save her.

Rab shut the door and hurried out, shivering as the cold air found every hole in his patched jacket and blew through his nightshirt to claw at his bones. His boots splashed through deep puddles as he raced across the yard, but when he reached the end of the farm track, there was no trace of Agnes to be found. She was gone.

He gazed up and down the lane, grinding his teeth in frustration. The moon was hidden behind thick cloud, and it was too dark to see more than a few paces in either direction. If he guessed wrong, then he might never catch up with Agnes. The thought chilled him even more than the bitter cold.

There was only one way to find her, one way to light up the night in a blinding flash of fire and fury. He pulled the hag stone from his pocket reluctantly, raising it once more to his eye.

Lightning zigzagged all around him, casting shadows across the wind-swept fields. On the road to Alloway, tall dark shapes in fluttering rags were urging on a smaller figure who stumbled along with a heavy blanket in her arms. Rab broke into a run, the stone clutched tight in his hand. As soon as it left his eye, he lost sight of the ghostly shapes, but he held the lantern aloft, praying the wind wouldn't find a way through the glass and snuff out the flickering candle before he could reach his sister.

He was out of breath by the time he caught up with her.

"Agnes!" Rab yelled, grabbing hold of her arm and spinning her round to face him. "Agnes, are you alright?"

His sister's eyes were open, but she was breathing so slowly it was clear she was in a deep sleep.

"Agnes! Wake up!" Even shaking her didn't help, but at least it reassured Rab that the precious bundle she was carrying was safe. Isabella started crying, trying to escape from the blanket she was trapped in. Rab was about to take her from Agnes, when something sharp cut across the back of his neck. He whirled round, but there was nothing there, only the night air whipping the hedgerows in the darkness.

Rab put a hand to his stinging neck, and when he drew it away, he saw a smear of blood on his palm. Pain flashed across his arm, then his back, and deep slashes appeared in his jacket, cutting through to his nightshirt.

No matter which direction Rab turned, he could see nothing in the road. He knew what was out there, though. And he knew there was only one way for him to see what was coming before he was cut to pieces.

He raised the hag stone to his eye.

At once his ears were filled with shrieking, and this time it wasn't just coming from the storm. A blur of shadows surrounded him and his sisters, red eyes glaring out from under hooded cloaks. Sharp claws sliced at the air around him, their gnarled fingers so old and withered they looked like the ancient branches of dying trees. Rab leapt back as another talon slashed at his face. The shadowy figures closed in, claws raised menacingly.

Rab had no weapons, so he used the only other thing he carried to defend himself. He swung the storm lantern at the figures, its weak flame guttering behind the glass. There was a horrible hissing sound as the shadows fell back, their claws twitching nervously at the sight of the small fire. Rab stepped closer to his sisters, holding the stone to his eye in one hand and brandishing the lamp in the other, daring the hooded figures to come any closer.

For a moment, Rab thought he had won. The figures stood still, their hissing dying to a murmur. Then the whispering grew louder, and Rab realised they weren't backing off and giving in.

They were summoning the wind.

Through the stone, Rab could see the gale picking up, ripping the dry leaves from the hedges and sending them whirling around him like the corpses of long-dead butterflies. Their sharp edges tore at Rab's hands, trying to force him to drop the stone and the lantern. He clung on grimly, raising the dim light higher and gritting his teeth as the leaves drew blood.

The rushing air found the tiny cracks in the old lantern's glass, and the candle inside flared and flickered, clinging desperately to life.

"No!" Rab gasped, watching in horror as a final gust extinguished the feeble flame, leaving only a trail of smoke behind. The hissing rose above the howling wind as the shadows closed in. Rab threw his arms around Agnes, shielding her and the baby from the claws that snatched at them.

There was an almighty shrieking noise, and Rab shut his eyes, waiting for the fatal blow to fall.

It never came.

Rab cautiously opened his eyes again.

The sun was rising in the east, casting a long ray of light across the fields. Slowly, he raised the hag stone once more.

The shadows were melting, disappearing like smoke. In an instant they were gone. Somewhere up in the treetops, the first birds began to wake, their dawn chorus drowning the last echoes of the shrieking figures.

It was over. They were safe.

"Agnes!" Rab shook his sleeping sister again. This time she opened her eyes, looking round groggily.

"Whit the...? Rab! Whit's going on?"

"You were sleep walking," Rab lied, biting his tongue

to stop himself from blurting out the truth. "You wandered out into the lane with Isabella."

"Oh, aye..." Agnes muttered, shaking her head as though waking up from a nightmare. "She must've been crying again. I must've been walking her up and down the kitchen and stepped out the door by mistake." She didn't sound very sure, but that was the story Rab was sticking with.

"Come on, let's get you back inside afore you freeze. You didnae even put your shoes on, you daft gowk."

Agnes looked down at her bare feet and shivered. Something told Rab it wasn't just the cold that was making her tremble.

Cousin Betty and her coven are no going to give up as easily as I thought, he frowned to himself as he led his sister back to the house. *Burning those dolls only did half the job. Now this cursed stone's back, I'm going to have to find a way to destroy it afore Halloween if I'm ever going to keep Agnes and Isabella out of harm's way.*

13

"Burning the dolls was no enough!" Rab sighed, slapping the hag stone down on the scullery table. "I need to get rid of this infernal thing for good."

Morven eyed the stone warily, looking almost as afraid of it as Rab did. "It's no easy to destroy something that powerful," she told him. "Fire's the best way to put a stop to magic, but it would take a deal of heat to even crack a hag stone."

"I tried dropping it in the fire at breakfast, but it didnae even get hot!"

"Ach, a wee kitchen flame will barely even tickle it. You need a real fire, Rab, one that can melt steel."

"You mean like a blacksmith's forge?" Rab asked eagerly. "There's a smithy in Purclewan. It's no too far—I could take it there!" Then his face fell. "Only, there's that much work to be done round the farm, I'll probably no get a chance to go afore Halloween. We've only got a few days left, but the wind's been that bad the farm buildings have been blown half to pieces. Will you take it to the forge for me, Morven?"

Morven's eyes narrowed till they were tiny slits, staring at the stone with such disgust Rab was scared he'd offended her.

"I know you dinnae like being mixed up in witchcraft again after whit happened to your family," he said quickly, "but I'm in sore need of your help."

"It's no that," Morven shook her head. "I've got a mountain of work to do round the house right now. Factor McNab's got worse, and it's set the whole family on edge. I've been shouted up the stairs more times today than I can count."

Rab frowned, glancing into the kitchen where the cook was fussing over pots on the stove and another maid was chopping vegetables. It looked like everyone was so preoccupied with their own work they barely even noticed Morven shirking in the scullery with him, let alone needed her to come running at a moment's notice.

Morven saw the doubt in his eyes, and she tried to reassure him. "Look, you'll get a chance to be rid of it in the next few days, I know you will. The main thing is making sure your family dinnae come down with fever afore Halloween like mine did."

"And how do I do that?" Rab asked. "I cannae stop Cousin Betty."

"Maybe no, but you can get rid of any more dolls she's made. They're whit cursed my family, remember? You've already destroyed two dolls and made sure Agnes and the baby willnae come down with the fever—you need to find the rest."

"But how? I saw Betty making them at her house, and if she's hidden them there then—"

"They willnae be at the cottage!" Morven rolled her eyes. She was starting to look impatient with his endless questions. "They need to be near the person they're cursing, or the spell willnae work. *Think*, Rab. Is there anywhere she might have hidden them at the farmhouse?"

Rab chewed his lip, trying to come up with a likely hiding place. Agnes and his mother kept everything neat as a pin, and they would've noticed if there'd been anything hidden in the parlour or kitchen. Besides, he hadn't let Cousin Betty out of his sight since he saw her making the dolls, she couldn't have hidden anything in the house without him noticing. Unless she hadn't hidden them *in* the house...

"I've got it!" Rab snapped his fingers and grinned in relief. "The other night I saw Cousin Betty standing in the yard by the water pump. I thought she'd just come up the lane, but now that I think on it, it looked more like she'd come from the barn. That must be where she's hidden them!"

"Then you've still got time, Rab. Find the rest of the dolls and destroy them, and that'll stop your family sickening like mine did." Morven's shoulders relaxed, and the tension drained from her face. Rab was touched by how much she seemed to care for his parents and siblings, even though she'd only known them a short while.

"But that still willnae protect Agnes and the baby from this wicked stone in the meanwhile," he frowned. "Every time it's turned up there's been trouble, and last night I only saved them from the witches by the skin of my teeth. You said the coven wants a baby to give to Old Nick at their Halloween ceremony," Rab frowned. "But whit do they want with Agnes?"

"They need new apprentices for their coven," Morven told him, "and they always choose young girls. Once they get their hands on your sister, they'll turn her to the dark side, and there'll be nothing you can do to save her."

Rab gulped. "Then I'll need to disobey Pa's orders to come straight back home after dropping off the rent. Ach! But how will I explain being away so long if I go to the smithy in Purclewan? Pa needs my help with the leaking byre roof, and he'll be right mad if I'm late."

"You can maybe afford to put it off a few days," Morven said, going to a drawer and rummaging around inside.

"After whit happened to Agnes and the baby last night?" Rab shook his head. "I have to destroy this thing as soon as I can."

"If you cannae take it to the forge afore Halloween,

you can maybe bind it so its powers willnae do any harm," Morven said, taking out a long length of what looked like thick brown string.

"Eh? Whit do you mean?"

"Ever since that misfortune befell my family, I've been learning all I can about witches, so I'll know how to protect myself and others from them," Morven whispered, checking to make sure the other maids were making too much noise in the kitchen for them to be overheard. "Here, bind the stone with this. Make sure you cover the whole eye, mind. That's where the power is."

Rab took the thick cord and began wrapping it carefully round the stone, binding it tightly so it couldn't slip off. "Whit is it?" he asked. "It doesnae feel like string."

"It's ivy vines, dried and dipped in mistletoe berry juice. There's nothing like it for tying magic to cursed objects so it cannae leak out and do harm."

"You think it'll be enough to stop the witches coming after Agnes and the baby?"

"Till Halloween, at least. Keep the stone on you, though, no more throwing it away or burying it. The witches will only send their familiars to fetch it, and the binding might slip off and give them a way through to you."

"Familiars?"

"You know—their creatures. Cats and dogs and the like."

"And birds?" Rab gulped, remembering the owl at his window.

"Aye, them too. Is it done?" She eyed the stone critically without touching it. Rab had covered it over with the long twists of ivy vine till the circular hole in the middle was completely covered. "That looks about right. Remember whit I said now—dinnae let it out of your sight until you get the chance to go to the forge. You've only got three days till—"

"Are you going to sit there all day gabbing, or are you going to get some work done?" the cook demanded, stomping in from the kitchen and glaring at Morven and the piles of unwashed dishes in the scullery sink.

"I was just getting started." Morven jumped up, throwing Rab an 'I told you so' look, and nodding at the door. Rab didn't need to be warned twice. He hurried out before the scowling cook could put him to work too. He had more than enough on his plate as it was.

He only hoped Morven would still be able to come to their house that night. Knowing she was there to help him when he needed her was the only thing keeping him going right now.

He put the bound stone back in his pocket, running all the way up the hill to Mount Oliphant.

The thunder clouds chased him back, but they didn't break that day. Louring over the farmhouse the whole afternoon, they turned the sky an ominous grey that slowly faded to black as night drew in.

"That's good work, boys, well done," their father said when it was too dark to continue working on the byre roof. "That should keep the rain off the cows, no matter how bad the coming storm gets."

"You think it'll break tonight, Pa?" Gil asked, pointing up at the thick clouds obscuring the moon.

"I think it's still gathering its strength. Can you feel the tension in the air, like the whole world's holding its breath? We can expect thunder and lightning this Halloween, there's no doubt about that. Pass the last straw bundle down, Rab. I'll stow it in the barn in case we get rain. Mind your step on the ladder, Gil, you'll get your supper a deal faster if you dinnae take a tumble."

They climbed carefully back down from the roof carrying their tools with them, eager to get back to the warmth of the kitchen and their waiting stew.

"I'll get those, Pa," Rab said. "You'd best go in and make sure Nannie hasnae set the kitchen on fire trying to make bannock bread again."

"Thanks, son." His father smiled at him gratefully and ruffled his hair before heading back to the farmhouse with Gil. Rab could see from the way his father's shoulders slumped how tired he was, but that wasn't why he'd offered to put the tools away. He quickly stowed the ladder and bundle of straw in the barn, carrying the basket of tools to the racks where the farm equipment was stored. He had to find Betty's dolls, and he didn't have much time.

Behind the threshers? No, she wouldnae put them near something we're always using. How about underneath the seed potatoes? Ach, they're no there either. Maybe they're with the old harnesses we havenae the money to repair yet...

Rab went through the barn as thoroughly as he could, but there was no trace of the other dolls Betty had made.

I'd best go in afore they wonder whit I'm up to out here, he thought, sighing in defeat. As he passed the sacks of newly threshed grain piled by the back wall, a loose floorboard creaked loudly under his foot.

Wait a minute!

He felt around the edges eagerly, searching for a way to prise it up. One end was loose and came away easily under his fingers. And there, lined up in a row in the hole underneath, were the rest of Cousin Betty's straw dolls.

Rab didn't have time to celebrate. He grabbed a spare sack and shoved them inside, hurrying round the back of the barn where the flames from his fire wouldn't be seen from the farmhouse window. He was so eager to get rid of the dolls his fingers trembled on the flint, and he struggled to strike a spark. Even in this sheltered spot, gusts of cold air rose up and swallowed the slightest flicker of light, until he was cursing in frustration.

If you dinnae light on this try, I'm going to take you all inside and dump the lot of you on the kitchen fire! he thought darkly, striking the firesteel against the flint again so sharply he almost dropped them. A spark flew out, catching the dry straw of his mother's figure. A small flame crackled to life, then the doll lit up in an orange glow. The fire spread quickly to the other dolls, and Rab heaved a sigh of relief as the cursed objects disintegrated into ashes and dust.

My family are safe from the fever, he grinned to himself. *Cousin Betty cannae touch them now.*

"Is that you, Rab?" a familiar voice sent a shiver of foreboding down his spine. He whirled round, tripping over his own feet in his haste to get away from the black-clad figure that loomed over him.

"Cousin Betty! Whit are you doing out here?" he gulped.

Betty Davidson gave him a long stare. Her old eyes were cloudy and yellow in the moonlight, but Rab had a horrible feeling they could still see right through him to his deepest, darkest secrets.

"The question is, Rab," she said sternly, "whit are *you* doing out here?"

14

"Ah, Rab, so you got rid of that lice-ridden pillow like I told you?" Morven said, stepping up suddenly behind Cousin Betty. Rab had never been so glad to see her.

"Whit? Er... oh, aye, I'll be having no more trouble on that score," Rab gulped, scattering the ashes of the fire with his boot and scratching his head as though there was something itchy in his hair.

"The lad's no got lice any more than you've got an honest heart," Betty muttered, glaring at Morven.

Before the maid could reply, Gil came running round the corner of the barn. "*There* you are, Rab," he panted, "I've been round the whole yard looking for you. Oh! Hello, Cousin Betty, Ma will be right pleased to see you're feeling better. Are you coming for supper as well, Morven?"

"I thought I'd give your ma a hand with the wee ones, seeing as how she's got so much work to do," Morven said, ignoring Betty's icy stare.

"There's no need for that now my arm's mended," Betty said frostily. "You'd be more use back at Doonholm, whit with the factor being ill and everything. You know, doing the job you're *paid* for?"

"Ach, they'll no miss her for a few hours," Gil grinned, settling the matter without realising he'd narrowly averted a war. "Come on, the supper's on the table and Pa's going to start gnawing on the table legs if you dinnae let him say prayers so we can eat."

He grabbed Betty's arm with one hand and Morven's arm with the other and led them both to the house before they could protest.

Rab felt certain the truce wouldn't last for long.

He was right. It lasted just until the supper had been eaten and Cousin Betty was putting the washed dishes away in the old wooden dresser.

"I'm right glad your arm's healed, Betty," Mrs Burns smiled. "I was getting worried about you down in that wee cottage on your own. Whit with the week we've had up here, we havenae had time to see to you, and I'm sorry about that."

"Dinnae worry, lass," Betty gave her a gap-toothed grin. "Nothing lays me low for long." She shot a sideways glance at Morven, who was busy playing with the children by the hearth, and her smile faded. "It was good of you to pitch in while I wasnae up to it, Morven," she said stiffly. "But now that I'm well again there's no need for you to waste your employer's time by coming up here anymore."

The cat-like stare Morven gave her was unreadable, but the meaning of her words was plain enough. "The Fergussons give me most evenings off, so I can spend them how I please."

"And are you no wasting your employer's money, taking food out their larder?" Betty pointed at the remains of the roast ham that Morven had brought up from the big house. The maid's cheeks went red, but it wasn't from embarrassment.

"If you're accusing me of theft, Betty Davison, then the stories about your wicked tongue are true. That joint was paid for out of my own pocket, and afore you stick your nose in, how I choose to spend my money is my own affair too."

"Och, Morven!" Mrs Burns protested, "I thought that joint was a gift from the Fergusson family. You didnae need to lay out your money for us, we're happy to have you to supper after all the help you've given me round the house."

"And I'm happy to give something in return after all the kindness you've shown me," Morven said. "If you willnae let me thank you in words, then let me give you wee things like this to show how much I appreciate you taking me in when I've no family of my own." She held up a large spool of white thread, slipping it into Mrs Burns's pocket before she could protest.

"The very thing I needed!" Mrs Burns beamed.

"Morven, you're a wee treasure."

"I thought it'd come in handy after Betty's clumsiness the other night cost you the jug of buttermilk to trade."

"Why, you wee snake-in-the-grass!" Betty's face went crimson with anger. "You know fine well it wasnae me who—"

Before William Burns could step in to end the quarrelling, the job was done for him by his namesake, Wee Willie.

"Cousin Betty, it's nearly Halloween," he reminded her. "You still havenae told us the story of the witches gathering, like you promised."

"You mean she hasnae told you it for at least five minutes now," his father grumbled. If there was one thing he liked less than Cousin Betty's stories, though, it was quarrelling. For once he let her sit by the hearth with the children in peace, going to the parlour with a book to study something more educational while she prattled.

As the children gathered round the old woman eagerly, Morven hovered nervously on the edge of the group, shooting Rab meaningful glances. He could only shrug back. He didn't know how to stop Cousin Betty boasting about her witches' exploits at Halloween without causing another argument, so he held his tongue. Morven rolled her eyes at him in disgust and went to make up the beds with fresh linen instead.

She knows how to make herself useful round here, he

thought, seeing his mother smile at the maid gratefully. *It's kind of her to let Ma have a wee rest, she's looking pale and worn out.*

He hoped it was only the heat of the fire, but there was a sheen of sweat on his mother's brow that hadn't been there before. But with two pairs of hands to help her round the house tonight, she looked more content rocking the baby than she had in a long while, so Rab turned his attention back to Cousin Betty, wondering what trouble she was going to stir up next.

"I'm going to tell you a Halloween tale you've no heard afore," Betty began, grabbing the children's attention right away. Nannie and Agnes exchanged excited glances, and Willie squirmed forward on Gil's lap to get closer. Even John stopped fiddling with Rab's socks and sat up to listen.

"This was told to me by my old friend, Tam, so I know every word of it is true."

Rab was pretty sure he'd never heard Betty mention a friend called Tam, but he was too scared of the old woman now to interrupt her.

"Fifty years ago, when he was young and carefree and a bit too fond of drink, he'd gone up to Ayr to do some market business. Well, he called it business, but he'd just been married a few months afore to a right wee shrew called Kate, and he was looking for an excuse to get out from under her thumb. I'm no saying he was much of a catch himself in those days, mind—he was a right blustering, drunken boaster, and I'd no have married him myself for all the silver in Scotland."

"You mean he didnae ask you?" Agnes smirked, too smart for her own good. Betty shot her a look, and she shut her mouth again double quick.

"After his business at market was over, Tam spent the rest of the day drinking, first with the miller, then with the blacksmith, and finally with the cobbler, till all of his money was spent. As night drew in and the storm began to rise, drowning out the sound of their merry singing, one by one Tam's companions began to slip away home, until all that was left at Tam's table was an empty ale mug and a bill he'd need an extra month in the year to work off."

"And that's how drink turns men into fools," William Burns called from the parlour, evidently listening despite pretending to have better things to do. "Rab and Gil—I hope the two of you will remember that in a few years when your friends all start egging you on to join them at the barstool."

Whit friends? Rab thought bleakly. *Even if we all survive this coming Halloween, there'll be nothing but farm work for us till we're old and grey.*

"Aye, Pa," he sighed.

"No, Pa," Gil chorused dutifully, eager to get back to Betty's tale and only half listening. "Ow! I mean, aye,

Pa!" he yelped when Rab's foot connected with his shin.

"Anyway..." Betty cleared her throat, gathering their attention again. "Tam was lucky that he had a fine mare waiting for him outside, as without that clever horse he'd never have got home that night. There was a wild storm blowing, the likes of which you've only seen in nightmares. The wind whistled down the chimneys, rattling the windows and howling as loud as the roaring thunder. The rain made the road so slick with mud his poor horse was more wading than trotting down the road. The Devil had a hand in that weather, Tam said, and I'm inclined to believe him."

The children shivered and drew closer to the fire.

"How did Tam know that?" Nannie whispered.

"Because he'd forgotten whit day it was until he passed the old kirk. Whit he saw there reminded him that it was All Hallows Eve—the night when witches' power is at its greatest, and they can break the chains holding fast the gates of hell."

"*Our* old kirk?" Gil gasped. "The one in Alloway?"

"The very same. Back then it was still in use, and the witches and warlocks were celebrating their success at opening the gates for their master to cross over for the night. They'd paid a hefty price for his passage to this world, though. The kirk was full of murderers' bones, a hanged thief, and the bodies of—"

"No the details, Betty!" Mrs Burns tutted. "Just give

the wee ones the gist of it."

It might have been the yellow light from the smoking tallow candles, but Rab thought his mother's face looked even paler in the gloom as the fire burnt lower.

"Aye, well, how they did it's no so important," Betty hurried on in case William Burns put down his book and came to put a stop to the story before she could finish it. "Whit mattered is whit their magic accomplished. The door to hell was open, and there was Old Nick himself in the form of a great black dog, playing the hornpipe with such a sinister shrieking that the very rafters rang with the hellish noise. The witches and demons were dancing with such whirling and birling and gnashing of teeth, it made Tam dizzy to watch them. Half-drunk as he was, he nearly slipped from his saddle, crying out as he grabbed at his reins."

Nannie gave a loud gasp and hugged Agnes tighter. "Did they hear him?" she asked, her eyes wide. "Did they come and drag him down to the underworld?"

"They tried," Betty said darkly, lowering her voice so they all had to lean in closer to hear. "The kirk went dark, and there was a sound like the angry buzzing of bees as the legions of hell poured into the kirkyard. Tam kicked his horse into the wildest gallop you ever did see and made for the bridge over the River Doon."

"Eh? Why did he ride to the Brig o' Doon?" Gil asked, earning him the glares of the other children for interrupting the story again. "Would he no have been better heading for one of the cottages in Alloway?"

"Aye, if he'd been a total fool, he might well have done that," Betty snorted. "Whit could a poor cottager do to save Tam from Old Nick? No, a drunk and a boaster Tam might have been, but he was no as daft as folk thought. He knew the one thing that witches cannae cross is running water. It drains their power, so if he could make it across the bridge then—"

Suddenly there came a loud crash, putting an end to Betty's storytelling.

Rab leapt up just in time to catch the baby as his mother crumpled to the floor. "Ma!" he gasped. "Whit's the matter?"

William Burns was back in the kitchen in an instant, lifting his wife onto the bed and feeling her forehead. Her face was ashen, and a trickle of sweat ran down her neck.

"She's burning up," he muttered. "Gil, go and fetch cold water from the pump."

"Maybe she sat too close to the fire?" Agnes fretted, rubbing her mother's hand and trying to turn the bloodless fingers pink again.

She was sitting further back than any of us, Rab frowned to himself. *Maybe she fell asleep and hit her head on the dresser. I'll ask Morven if she saw*—He turned round, but the maid was nowhere to be seen. He was about to check the yard, when he saw a figure climbing up the stairs to the loft. "Morven? Whit are you doing up there?"

"I was going to change the sheets on your bed, Rab," she called down. "Your ma looked tired tonight, so—"

"Never mind the linen," Rab told her, "get down here right away! Ma's taken sick all of a sudden."

Morven hurried down, dumping her armful of linen on the table and taking the bowl of cold water that Gil brought. She dipped a handkerchief into it, but before she could wipe the sweat off Mrs Burns's brow, Betty snatched it off her.

"You've 'helped' enough for one night, you wee minx. Get yourself back home and leave us in peace. I'll look after my cousin tonight. You'll no mind me staying over, will you William?"

"If you would I'd be grateful," Rab's father nodded, his brows knitting in worry as Betty tucked blankets around his wife who was now shivering as though she was cold.

"I'm happy to stay to help too," Morven protested. "I could—"

"That's much appreciated, but you've a job to get up for, and I'll no have the Fergussons inconvenienced on my account," William said. "Besides, are you no needed to nurse the factor? I hear he hasnae improved. Nip back home afore it gets too late and the doors are all locked up, there's a good lass."

Morven couldn't argue with his direct command. She wrapped her shawl around her shoulders, gave the children a kiss each, and walked out into the night, dragging her feet unwillingly the whole way. Rab hurried out after her.

"Dinnae go!" he cried. "Dinnae leave us all in Cousin Betty's clutches!"

"I cannae stay, Rab, your father made that clear. There's nothing more I can do here tonight."

"But—"

"Keep your voice down or she'll hear you!" Morven hissed, glancing nervously at the door.

"Is it the sickness?" Rab whispered, squeezing her arm so hard to stop her going he was afraid he'd leave a mark. "Is it whit your family had?"

Morven nodded, her eyes glittering like emeralds in the darkness.

"Then whit can I do?" Rab had to fight to keep his voice from breaking. His family were in mortal danger, and he'd never felt so afraid in all his life. "You said burning the dolls would keep them safe!"

"I'm sorry, Rab, but Betty's magic must be too powerful," Morven told him. "There's only one thing left for you to try now."

"Whit?" Rab demanded.

"You're no going to like it."

"I dinnae care whit I have to do, just tell me!"

"No tonight, there's no time. Come by the big house tomorrow, we can make a plan then." Morven shook off his arm and hurried up the lane.

"But whit'll I do in the meantime?" Rab called after her.

Morven looked back, her black curls whipping around her face in the breeze. "The only thing you can do, Rab," she said ominously. "Pray."

Rab gulped hard and turned back to the house where a witch was weaving her magic over his sick mother. He was sure it would take more than prayers to save his family now.

15

Rab was right. Sitting up all night, praying with all his might, was no help at all. In fact, it only seemed to make matters worse.

He sat by the hearth with his father as the hours ticked by, keeping his eye on Betty Davidson as she bathed his mother's brow with cold water, and making sure she didn't mutter anything that sounded like magic.

By the time the clock on the mantelpiece chimed four in the morning, all of the children were long asleep, and his father dozed in his chair, unable to keep his eyes open any longer. Rab kept his own eyes trained on Cousin Betty, closing them only for a moment when the weight of his lids became too much to bear...

He awoke with a start, the sound of the cock crowing cutting through his troubled dreams. "Is she better?" he asked, rubbing his aching eyes and stumbling over to the wall bed where his mother lay.

"No, Rab, it's worse than I thought."

Cousin Betty wasn't sitting by his mother's side, but kneeling on the small boys' trundle bed, mopping their damp foreheads with a cloth. Wee Willie and John were tossing and turning in their sleep, sweat soaking through their nightshirts.

Nannie was curled up next to his mother in the big bed, her face just as pale and her hair clinging to her fevered brow.

"No the wee ones too!" Rab gasped. "Pa! Wake up! Nannie and the boys are..." He trailed off, seeing the waxy sheen on his father's face as he slept fitfully by the fire. Rab shook him hard, but his father slumped forward, his head hanging dangerously close to the hearth's glowing embers.

"Wake up, Pa!" Rab urged. "I cannae manage this without you!"

There was nothing Rab could do. The sickness had got hold of both his parents, and his younger siblings were caught tightly in the grip of Betty's magical fever.

"Where's Agnes and the baby?" he demanded, almost adding, *Whit have you done with them, you wicked old hag?* But he bit his tongue before it came out. He was powerless against the witch on his own, and he couldn't risk making her angry.

"They're fine," Betty tried to reassure him. "Agnes is walking the baby around in the yard—wee Isabella's crying was making the boys even more restless."

Two of his sisters were safe at least, for now. But what about...?

"GIL!" Rab yelled, already halfway up the loft stairs before Betty could call him back.

"Gil! Are you—"

"Argh!"

Rab collided with his brother at the top of the ladder, grabbing hold of him to stop them both from tumbling to the floor.

"Whit's wrong, Rab? Is Ma...?" Gil couldn't bring himself to finish the question.

"She's the same as last night," Rab said before Gil got the wrong idea. "But everyone else is sick—Pa, Nannie and the boys. Only Agnes and the baby are alright. And Cousin Betty, of course," he added darkly.

"Pa's sick and all? Then whit are we going to do?" Gil asked, looking to his big brother to solve the problem.

Rab took a deep breath. He was in charge now. It was up to him to save his family.

"Saddle Bonny—she's the fastest horse—and ride as hard as you can for Doctor Campbell. I'll head to Doonholm to fetch Morven."

"Eh? Whit's she got to do with it?" Gil frowned.

"Her family died of a fever, remember? She might know something about it."

"Oh... right." Gil didn't look convinced, but he followed his brother's orders anyway, getting ready in a flash and running out to the fields. Rab didn't have time to tell him the whole story. He had to get to Morven.

She'd said there was one thing left to try, and he had to find out what that was.

"Agnes!" he called, running into the yard with his bootlaces flapping and his jacket half on. "Are you both alright?"

"Aye, but we four and Cousin Betty are the only ones," his sister sniffed, trying to wipe away the tears from her cheeks before Rab could see them.

"Dinnae cry, pet," Rab soothed, giving her a hug and kissing the sleeping baby gently. "We'll get this sorted out. Gil's going for the doctor, and I'm going to get help from Morven. I need you to be strong and look after our parents and the wee ones while we're gone, can you do that?"

Agnes gave a last sniff and nodded bravely.

"And make sure you keep an eye on Cousin Betty. Watch whit she does, and dinnae let her out of your sight, do you understand?"

"Why?" Agnes frowned. "She's been more help than any of us."

"Aye, but..." Rab hesitated, trying to come up with a believable excuse. "But... she's old, and she's already been up all night. I dinnae want her exhausting herself. At her age, it might be dangerous. She might get confused and give the wee ones something that'll make them sick, instead of medicine. So keep a close watch on her, alright?"

Agnes nodded again, even more determined this time, and hurried back into the house with the sleeping baby.

Rab was just heading for the lane when a shout from the near field stopped him in his tracks.

"Rab! Come here, quick!"

Rab hurried over, skidding to a stop when he saw what had happened. The two strong plough horses, Bonny and Thistle, were lying on their sides, their eyes rolling and their skin slick with sweat. The fever had spread, and even the animals on the farm weren't safe from it.

Rab swore and kicked one of the fenceposts in frustration. "Right, you'll have to ride to Ayr on Meg, Gil. I put her in the byre last night to keep her warm."

"That old bag of bones?" Gil's eyebrows shot up. "She'll die of exhaustion afore we even reach the town. I'll run to the next farm and ask to borrow one of their horses. They willnae begrudge us for something so important."

"Good lad," Rab grinned as Gil raced off. At least he didn't have to deal with this all on his own.

He hesitated as he passed the byre, then grabbed an armful of tack to saddle up Meg himself. Running down to Doonholm might be quicker, but he'd had a restless night, and he wasn't sure when he'd next get another good sleep. He needed to save all the strength he could.

He was regretting his decision by the time Meg

trotted lazily down the back lane to the big house. No matter how many times Rab kicked her or cracked the reins, Meg wouldn't go a step faster than a slow jog. Rab suspected it was her idea of payback for him forgetting to bring her a carrot or a handful of oats since their last outing.

"Sorry I've no brought you any treats for a while, lass," he said, giving her neck a pat, "but I've had a lot on my mind recently. Can you no go a wee bit faster?"

Meg dutifully picked up her pace, but before Rab could wonder if she actually did understand his words, he realised she was heading for the familiar figure who was hanging out the washing in the servants' yard.

"Morven! I'm right glad to see you. Things have got so bad at home I'm half scared to go back in case the worst has happened while I'm gone."

"Whit do you mean?" The maid looked up at him, her eyes reflecting the worry in his.

"It's no just Ma—Pa and the wee ones are all sick too! Except for Gil, Agnes and the baby, I mean," he added quickly. He knew how fond she was of Agnes and Isabella, and he didn't want her fretting about them. "I tried to stay awake all night to watch Cousin Betty, but I must've nodded off for a few hours. That's when she wove her wicked magic! When I woke up, they were all sick with the fever."

"Then it's as bad as I feared, and there's only one thing

left you can do now to stop her," Morven said darkly, reaching into her pinafore and pulling out a corked bottle. "Here, take this."

"Whit is it?"

"Your last hope. Betty's too powerful a witch to stop any other way. Put that in her tea and make sure she drinks it."

"Whit'll it do to her?" Rab asked, taking the bottle as gingerly as if he'd been offered a rattlesnake. "It's no poison, is it?" He took the cork out and gave the liquid inside a suspicious sniff. It smelled sharp, with a faint hint of nightshade and holly berry.

"Of course it's no!"Morven rolled her eyes. "You think I'd ever want to hurt anyone? It's a sleeping draught. Mrs Fergusson uses opium for her nerves, and I stole some of her tonic and mixed it with a few things to make it stronger. It'll no do Betty any harm, but it'll knock her out cold for two whole days. If you give it to her now, she'll sleep right through Halloween tomorrow."

"And she'll no be able to meet with her witches and make mischief!" Rab grinned. "Morven, you're a genius! You think that will be enough to break the spell she's cast on my family?"

"Aye, now that you've burnt all her dolls, it should be enough," Morven reassured him. "Here's a few sugar lumps." She handed them up to him in a small square of brown paper. "You can hide the taste of the draught with them. Now get going. Factor McNab's taken another turn for the worse. He's at death's door, and Doctor Campbell's been sent for, so I have lots to see to here."

"Ach, then Gil's been sent on a wild goose chase to Ayr for him," Rab frowned. "It cannae be helped. Will you send the doctor over when he's done here?"

"Aye, if he's willing," Morven said hesitantly. They both knew that a rich family like the Fergussons and their sick factor would take priority over a poor farming family like Rab's. "I'm sorry I cannae come today, but I'll do my best to slip out tomorrow, if I can," she said, giving his hand a squeeze.

Rab smiled back, trying not to let the tears welling up in his eyes show. He was tugging on the reins to head home, when he turned back suddenly. "Woah, Meg. Morven—you said that Betty wouldnae be able to make mischief when she was asleep because all her dolls have been burned?"

"Aye," Morven nodded.

"But whit about the other dolls?"

"Whit other dolls?"

"The ones in the old kirk."

"WHIT?"

Morven's green eyes flashed in anger, and Rab realised he'd made a big mistake. He'd been so busy worrying about the hag stone and the dolls shaped like his family, he'd forgotten to tell Morven about the ones he'd seen

Cousin Betty put in the ruined church. He filled her in as fast as he could, telling her about the woven images of witches and the Devil that stared out of the crumbling windows and door. By the time he'd finished, Morven's lips were drawn up into a tight line, and her fists were clenched so hard he thought she might explode.

"And did you no think to tell me all this afore now?" she snapped.

"Sorry, Morven, but I've had a lot on my mind of late," Rab said meekly. "I didnae think those wee dolls were as important as—"

"No important?" Morven stamped her foot, her teeth gnashing so hard Rab was afraid they were going to crack. "You wee fool! Those are her summoning spells! If you dinnae go there right now and burn them, then her coven will still be able to gather on Halloween without her."

"Whit, now? But I've got so much else to do! I still havenae had a chance to get to the smithy with this awful stone that's been weighing my pocket down for days. And with my family all sick, I—"

"Rab Burns!" Morven glared at him, her eyes flashing. "Do you want your family to end up like mine? Do you want to lose them all tomorrow cause you couldnae be bothered stopping the coven from gathering and weaving their wicked spells?"

"Of course I dinnae! But the kirk's only up the road, could you no—"

"When would I have time for it?" Morven cut him off before he could finish. "I've already been in trouble this morning for taking time out of chores to make up that draught for you." She pointed at the bottle Rab had slipped into his saddle bag. "If I'm seen shirking off again, I'll no be able to visit you to make sure everything's going to plan. Do you want to stop the witchcraft before tomorrow night or no?"

"I dinnae want you to think I'm no grateful for all your help," Rab said quickly. "I'm just fretting, is all. I'll go straight to the kirk and get the dolls burned, then I'll head back to dose Cousin Betty up. You can count on me, Morven. Together we're going to put a stop to Cousin Betty's coven gathering."

"That's good to hear." Morven's scowl gave way to a smile, her face losing its harsh edges and glowing with beauty again. "I'm on your side, Rab, remember that."

"Aye, I will. Thank you!" Rab called over his shoulder as he nudged Meg into a trot and set off down the drive. He might not have his parents to help him, or much time to act, but at least he had Morven to guide him along this strange path of witchcraft and devilry he'd stumbled upon.

16

The wind was whispering through the trees in the kirkyard. The anguished creaking and groaning of branches unsettled Meg so badly she wouldn't take a single step off the lane. Rab had to tie her to the remains of the gatepost and venture into the graveyard by himself.

The whirling air had stripped the last of the dead leaves from the branches, and Rab shuddered as he gazed up through the twisted wood. The storm clouds were gathering in ever thicker knots in the sky above, their grey edges bulging ominously with the weight of rain and thunder.

Looks like it's no just the witches who are gathering for Halloween, he thought. *That storm looks like it'll be every bit as wild as the one in Betty's story.*

His hands tightened into fists at the thought of the old witch boasting about her coven's meeting to his brothers and sisters, his anger lending him courage as he stepped over the fallen gravestones and approached the ruined church.

I'll put a stop to all your mischief and wipe the smug

smile off your toothless face, Betty Davidson, he vowed.

But when he saw the image of the Devil staring up at him from the old kirk threshold, his heart starting thumping hard in his chest and his legs began to wobble. Maybe it was the way the straw was woven, or a trick of the dim light, but the huge dog seemed to be sneering at him. Taking a deep breath, Rab stepped over it, his boots brushing the doll's plaited ear horns. He knew he had to get this job done fast or he'd lose his nerve altogether.

The flagstones beneath his feet were loose and cracked, and he stumbled, grabbing for a clump of ivy on the wall. It came away in his hands, the thick tendrils pulling chunks of crumbling stone down as they were tugged loose. The whole interior of the kirk was so overgrown it was hard to see in the dim light, and Rab used the snaking ivy vines as a rope to guide him in the darkness.

The first window he came to had a witch doll sitting on the sill, its hooked nose and broomstick unmistakeable in the gloom. Rab snatched it up and shoved it in the sack he'd found in Meg's saddle bag, unwilling to touch the hideous thing for one second longer than he had to.

The wind suddenly picked up, whistling sharply through the branches overhead as though in warning. Rab looked up. A few rotting rafters were all that remained of the original roof, jutting out of the surrounding walls like broken ribs. They were covered in a tangled mass of vegetation so thick it was like a living, breathing curtain that whispered and sighed with each puff of air. Rab shivered and kept going.

The next window contained an even scarier creature, its horns and claws extended as though reaching out for Rab. He stuffed it in the sack so fast he nearly dropped it. The breeze blew harder still, catching at his collar and nipping at his fingers. He ignored the sinister omen, continuing round each of the windows until the sack was full of straw dolls. By the time he'd finished, the wind was roaring in the treetops, the rotting timbers in the remains of the roof shuddering in their wall joints.

But there was one doll left that he was too afraid to touch. He dumped the sack down on the threshold beside the woven image of the Devil, and pulled the tinderbox from his jacket pocket.

Lucky I left this in here after burning the dolls by the barn last night, he thought, *or I'd be in a rare fix now with no way to light this lot.*

Luck wasn't on his side now, though. The howling wind seemed determined to stop him, every spark whipped away before it could reach the pile of woven dolls. There was no way Rab was ever going to get a fire lit out in the open. He looked round, searching for somewhere more sheltered. Inside the old kirk would be no good—the gathering storm was rushing through the windows and the hole where the roof had been. There would be no shelter in there. Most of the gravestones had toppled over, and the ones that remained upright were too exposed to offer much protection from the wind sweeping the kirkyard.

I cannae take them home with me! he thought desperately. *Cousin Betty would find out whit I was up to in a flash if I burned them behind the barn again.*

Rab had almost given up hope when he caught sight of the small building at the back of the churchyard.

Of course! The mausoleum! It'll be sheltered enough in there.

He grabbed his sack, hesitating for only a moment before picking up the Devil doll by the end of a horn, and dashed over to the old monument. Inside it was blacker than ever, and Rab could barely see past the rusting bars that guarded its entrance. He didn't need to get inside himself, though. He stuffed the straw Devil through the bars, dropping it onto the stone floor on the other side. One by one, the rest of the dolls in the sack followed, until they were piled up like a mini bonfire.

This had better work, Rab thought, or *I'm all out of ideas.*

Carefully, he stretched his arms through the metal bars, and struck the flint with the firesteel. A spark flew up, catching the edge of a witch's broomstick. At once the straw began to smoke, the ends curling and glowing red.

Come on! Catch! Rab willed the little flame to fight for life as the storm rose to a screech. It whipped round Rab, blowing his sack away and nearly bowling him over, but he clung grimly to the bars of the mausoleum, his eyes fixed on the small fire that was beginning to rise inside. The wind couldn't reach it. Smoke curled up from the pile of dolls, and in another instant they'd caught fire, the smell of burning straw filling the kirkyard.

The flames threw eerie shadows on the walls of the burial chamber, ghostly outlines of claws, horns and cloven hooves dancing across the stone. Rab gasped and blinked, and in another second the images were gone.

He rubbed his eyes and looked again, but the fire had gone out, and all that was left of the dolls was a pile of grey ashes drifting in the breeze. The storm had died down again, the kirkyard as quiet now as the graves themselves.

Somehow the silence was more unsettling than the uncanny howling had been. Rab jumped to his feet and bolted back to the safety of the lane and his waiting horse.

"Home, Meg!" he ordered, leaping into the saddle and giving her a kick. She took off at a canter, every bit as eager to leave the kirkyard behind as Rab was. Her legs weren't up to the challenge of the hill, though, and she slowed to a trot, then a stumbling walk as the path got steeper. Halfway up, Rab had to get off, cursing his decision to bring her in the first place.

By the time he'd turned Meg loose in the fields and run back to the house, he was panting just as hard as the old horse.

"Agnes!" he shouted, almost pulling the door off its hinges in his rush to get inside. "Agnes! Is everyone—"

"Rab!" Cousin Betty grabbed his arm, making him jump. "Shh!" She put a finger to her lips. "The poor wee lass is worn out and needs a nap. I've finally got the baby back to sleep again, so if you wake either of them, I'll skin you alive!"

It was the same threat Betty made to all the children when she thought they weren't behaving themselves, but hearing it now made Rab's flesh crawl.

He hurried over to the wall bed to make sure she hadn't done anything else to his family. Agnes was curled up at the bottom in a blanket, but unlike their mother and Nannie, whose faces were deathly pale and whose breath came out in short gasps, Agnes's cheeks were still rosy pink. Rab only relaxed slightly when he saw the baby was sleeping peacefully in her cradle too. The rest of his family were still feverish, his father twitching and muttering to himself in his chair by the fire, but at least Betty hadn't harmed Agnes and Isabella while he was gone.

"Where have you been, Rab?" Betty demanded. "I've been needing you these past two hours!"

I bet you have, Rab thought darkly, *so you can put me under your evil spell too.* He tried not to let the suspicion show on his face, giving her an apologetic look instead and reciting the excuse he'd been practising all the way up the hill. "I went down to Doonholm, to see Morven and—"

"Whit! You've no been chasing after that wee minx of a maid when your family are all in need of nursing, have you?" Betty's scowl grew so deep her eyes were nearly crossed.

"No! I sent Gil off to Ayr this morning to fetch Doctor Campbell, but with Factor McNab still sick himself, I thought it was best to check down at Doonholm to see if the doctor was there instead. Turns out the Fergussons had already sent for him, so I left a message telling him to call on us as soon as he was done at the big house."

"Ah." Betty's face relaxed, and she gave him a pat on the shoulder. "You're a smart lad, Rab, that was quick thinking. It'll be good to get the doctor's opinion on this fever—I've never seen anything like it."

Rab shrunk from her touch, her false words ringing hollow in his ears. He'd managed to fool a witch, though, and that gave him hope that he could trick her into drinking Morven's sleeping draught. With Agnes resting and Gil still away on his errand, it was now or never.

"Have a wee seat by the fire, Cousin Betty, you must be puffed out by now. I'll fetch some water and make us a cup of tea. There's some scones left over from supper last night—it's no much, but it'll do us for dinner."

"Thanks, Rab," Betty gave him a toothless grin and settled into the chair opposite his sleeping father, sighing as the weight was eased from her aching bones. Rab almost felt sorry for her, but one look at his father's bloodless lips and sweating brow was enough to snuff out the flicker of guilt over what he was about to do.

He filled the tea kettle at the pump, putting it on the fire and keeping an eye on Betty while it heated. She was resting her eyes, but he had the odd feeling the old witch was able to watch him through her lids as he poured Morven's draught into a mug.

Dinnae chicken out now, he told himself, trying to keep his nerve. His hands were shaking so hard he spilled some of the sleeping draught on the floor. *She's a witch, no a mind reader. Just act natural, and she'll no suspect a thing.*

He lifted the steaming tea kettle as casually as he could, adding some milk to the mugs and pulling out the sugar Morven had given him. He carefully stirred the three lumps into Betty's mug, hoping the sweetness would mask the bitter taste of the sleeping draught.

Finally, he carried the mugs over to Betty, nudging her awake again and making sure he passed her the right one. So she wouldn't get suspicious, he drew up a stool beside her and took a big swig from his own mug.

"Thanks, Rab, this is just whit I needed," she sighed, blowing on the steaming tea to cool it.

Rab held his breath.

Betty took a big gulp of tea, and her eyes narrowed. Rab's hair nearly stood on end when she demanded, "Whit in the name of goodness have you put in that, Rab?"

"Um... whit do you mean?" he asked, his voice quavering.

"It's sweeter than one of the baker's buns. Where did you get the sugar from?"

"Er... from the big house," Rab answered truthfully.

"No from Morven?" Betty looked horrified. "Anything that comes from that thieving wee toad's bound to come at a price!"

"No, of course it wasnae from her!" Rab said before Betty could spit the tea out and set her mug down. "The cook gave it to me when she saw me in the kitchen. She can be kind sometimes, when she's no in a sour mood. And she hasnae forgotten all the good work Pa did when he looked after their gardens for them."

"Oh, well, that's different." Betty swallowed the tea and took another big gulp.

Rab hid his sigh of relief, taking a sip of tea and wondering how long Morven's potion would take to work. He was going to look for the leftover scones, when Cousin Betty said something very strange.

"Now, lad, you're a wee bit older than the others, and with your ma and pa so sick, you're the one I'm going to have to trust with this secret."

"Whit secret?" Rab said suspiciously. *Surely she's no going to come right out and admit to whit she's been up to?*

"You know the stories I've been telling of witches gathering on Halloween?" she continued, swallowing another mouthful of tea. "Well, they're all true. I've no been making them up."

She's admitting it! Rab gasped to himself. *Does she think she can sweet-talk me into helping with her wicked plans?* He stared at Betty in amazement, wondering what on earth she was going to say next.

"That story about Tam and the old kirk—do you remember it?"

"Aye," Rab nodded.

"Well, tomorrow marks fifty years to the very night that gathering took place. From all the signs I've been seeing—the direction the wild geese have been flying and the way the ivy's been growing thicker in the kirkyard to ward off the evil—I'm sure the coven's coming back to that very spot to mark the anniversary tomorrow night." Betty words were slightly slurred, and she blinked hard as though to clear her vision.

"You think the witches are going to gather in the old kirk in Alloway tomorrow night?" Rab asked, trying to act like the news was a surprise. "How? I mean, do they no have to be summoned or something?"

Betty blinked again, slower this time, as though she was having trouble keeping her eyes open. "Aye," she said sleepily, "they do. They have to be summoned by a witch who walks among the living. And..." she yawned, "we have a... a witch living among... among us right... here..."

"Who?" Rab asked with bated breath. He wanted to hear Betty's confession come from her own lips, but her eyes closed, and her grip loosened, the mug of drugged tea slipping to the floor before Rab could catch it. Betty slumped back in her chair, her snores loud enough to wake the dead.

At least they're no loud enough to summon her coven for tomorrow night, Rab thought in relief.

He mopped up the spilled tea, then sat back to wait for Betty's magic to wear off and his family to recover now that the witch had finally been put out of action.

17

By late afternoon the next day, Rab was still waiting for his family to get better.

"I thought you said dosing Betty up with that potion would stop her mischief and end my family's fever!" he complained to Morven when she finally managed to slip away and run up to Mount Oliphant.

"I didnae say that, Rab," she whispered back, checking to make sure Gil was out seeing to the sick horses and Agnes was filling up another bowl of cold water by the pump. "I said it would stop her summoning her coven at Halloween tonight. The fever's taken such a strong hold, the magic willnae be stopped by sending the old witch to sleep."

"You dinnae mean that we have to...?" Rab gulped, nodding at Cousin Betty still snoring by the fire.

"The thing you need to get rid of is that hag stone you've been lugging around. You were meant to take it to the smithy ages ago," Morven snapped. She seemed to be in an awful rush today, and Rab felt guilty that she was so worried about getting caught shirking and punished by the Fergussons on his account.

"I know, but I didnae want to leave my family, no with them all so sick," Rab sighed. "I've been waiting since yesterday for Doctor Campbell to come, but he's no been yet. Did you no pass on my message?"

"Aye, I did, Rab, and he says he'll come afore supper today. There's no much he can do for Factor McNab now anyway."

"You mean he's going to...?"

Morven nodded gravely, and Rab clenched his fists. "Then Cousin Betty's curse killed him. I have to get rid of this evil thing afore my family is next."

He pulled the stone bound with ivy from his pocket, its sinister coldness burning his palm as he held it up. Morven shuddered and stepped back at the sight of it.

"Put that thing away," she hissed, "I cannae stand to look at it."

Rab thrust it back in his pocket, but he could still feel the icy weight against his leg through his thin breeches.

"You need to get rid of it right now; you cannae wait any longer," Morven warned.

"Should I no wait for Doctor Campbell first? He might be able to—"

"There's nothing a medical man can do against magic!" Morven scowled, growing more impatient with him. Seeing his face fall, her eyes softened. "Listen, that fever might be caused by magic, but it'll spread just like a regular illness. It's a wonder none of the rest of you have caught it by now."

"You mean me and Gil and Agnes and the baby might catch it?"

"Aye, with the baby being so wee, she's most at risk. You need to keep them out of this house till you've dealt with the stone and put a stop to all this wickedness once and for all."

"But where can Isabella go?" Rab frowned. "Ma would have sent her to Cousin Betty's, but now..." he trailed off, glancing at the old witch sleeping by the fire. "Maybe I can get Agnes to take her down to the cottage and look after her there for the night?"

"That's no a good idea. Who knows whit magic charms and cursed objects Betty's got lying around in there? It wouldnae be safe." Morven shook her head. She bit her lip, thinking hard, then came up with another suggestion. "I should take the baby back to Doonholm for the night. Agnes could come with me and look after her. Mrs Fergusson wouldnae mind me keeping them in my room for just one night, no when she hears from the doctor how sick the rest of your family are."

"Are you sure?" Rab said doubtfully.

"Aye, it's for the best," Morven said decisively. "Agnes?" she called. "Put that bowl down, pet, and go and pack a bag. It's best if you bring the baby and come to stay with me tonight."

"But whit about Ma and Pa and the wee ones?" Agnes looked half worried, half pleased at the invitation. "Who'll look after them?"

"Rab and Gil will take care of everything here. The doctor's coming soon, and he'll put everyone to rights. By the time you return tomorrow, things will be back to normal, or near enough. But in the meantime, you need to get the baby away—whit would your ma say if she woke up and found wee Isabella had caught the fever too?"

"I hadnae thought of that!" Agnes gasped. She ran to fetch a travelling bag and began hastily shoving clothes into it along with a spare blanket for Isabella. She was packed before Rab could come up with a good reason to stop her. The hag stone in his pocket was burning so cold against his leg it was making it hard for him to think.

"Are you sure everything will be alright here?" Agnes asked Rab, looking round the rest of the sleeping family members doubtfully.

"Aye, it'll all work out fine," Rab reassured her, wishing he could put his finger on the nagging doubt that was tugging at the back of his mind. "Hurry now, the storm's about to break, and I dinnae want to see the baby caught in it."

"She'll be safe with me," Morven smiled, lifting Isabella from her crib and holding on to her tightly as she hustled Agnes to the door. Her white teeth glittered in the firelight as she said a quick goodbye, and then she was gone, hurrying Agnes down the lane with her black curls twisting restlessly in the breeze.

"Where are they going?" Gil came running across the yard just in time to see the figures disappearing in the distance.

"Morven's taking Agnes and Isabella to Doonholm, to make sure they dinnae catch the fever afore Doctor Campbell's had a chance to come and cure it."

"Oh. And where are you going?" He raised an eyebrow when he saw that Rab had laced his boots and was pulling on his jacket.

"I need to run an errand," Rab said, setting off before Gil could stop him. "Look after things here till Doctor Campbell comes—he willnae be long," he called back. "There's a bowl of water by the bed, make sure you keep everyone's brow nice and cool, but dinnae take their blankets off."

"But...!" Gil's protests faded as Rab broke into a run, heading down the road towards Purclewan. He hated leaving his little brother to nurse his sick family all on his own, but the only way to break the spell was to get rid of the hag stone once and for all.

Even though there was another hour at least until sunset, the sky was as grey as ashes, the clouds knotted so tight overhead that not a trace of daylight could break through. The air was humming with the expectation of thunder, the torrents of pent-up rain ready to fall at any moment. With the wind at his back, Rab was half carried along to Purclewan by the strong gusts that raked the fields and stripped the last of the crackling leaves from the hedgerows.

By the time he got to the blacksmith's cottage, Rab was so out of breath he had to lean on the pump to stop himself falling over in the gale. The wind snatched the air from his lungs, and his legs trembled with the effort to stay upright. The hag stone seemed to get heavier with every step he took, and he wondered if it knew what he was planning to do with it.

Whine all you want, you nasty piece of work, Rab thought, pulling it from his pocket and staring at it in disgust. *You're going in the smithy's forge whether you like it or no.*

He was so busy trying to catch his breath and thinking what a relief it would be to finally get rid of the stone, that at first he didn't notice something was wrong. Then it dawned on him what was so different about the blacksmith's yard today, and his heart dropped to the bottom of his boots.

The place was deserted, the forge cold and dead as the kirkyard at Alloway.

No! Rab gasped, staring round in confusion. *It cannae be closed today! The smithy must be here somewhere!*

He ran to the small cottage attached to the forge,

pounding on the door loud enough to rouse Henry McCandlish and his wife even if they were sleeping in their graves. There was no answer. When Rab peered through the small kitchen window, he could see that their fire wasn't lit despite the chill in the air.

"Are you looking for the smithy, lad?" a voice called.

Rab turned to see a labourer sticking his head out of a nearby cottage door.

"Aye! Is he no well?"

"He's well enough, he's just no here, is all. He got word this morning that a relative's passed away, so the family have gone to Monkton for a few days for the funeral. If you're needing work done urgently you can always go to the blacksmith in Ayr."

"Oh," Rab said in a small voice, adding, "thanks!" before the door closed again. He stood alone in the empty yard, staring at the hag stone in his hand, and feeling his whole world crumbling around him. He couldn't destroy the stone now. Even if he had the energy to run all the way to Ayr, the forge there would be closed up for the night by the time he arrived.

He couldn't stop the stone's magic with fire and save his family that way.

All he could do now was head home and hope he could come up with another plan before the fever claimed his parents and siblings the way it had claimed Morven's family five Halloweens ago.

18

"Rab! Where have you been? You look like you've been dragged through a ditch backwards and drowned in the duck pond!" Gil gasped when Rab finally staggered through the door.

The skies had opened up as Rab was leaving the empty forge, the driving rain making every step home a huge effort. By the time he got back, it was dark, the thunder pealing ominously in the distance. The storm was rolling closer as night drew in.

"Never mind me," Rab muttered, throwing his soaking jacket in a heap and rummaging around in a drawer for a dry shirt. "How are things here?"

"No good," Gil frowned. He was sitting on the edge of the trundle bed, mopping John's brow and soothing Willie who was tossing and turning in his sleep. "You just missed Doctor Campbell. He's left some medicine, but he says there's no much we can do but wait it out."

"I hope he didnae charge for telling us whit we already knew!" Rab said in disgust, moving his father's chair a little further from the fire and grabbing another cloth to wipe the sweat from his forehead. He wasn't angry with the doctor, he was angry with himself. If he'd only taken the hag stone to the forge yesterday, his family might have recovered by now.

"He doesnae know whit's up with Cousin Betty, though," Gil looked puzzled. "He says she's no sick, but she's no waking up either. Do you think it's something serious, Rab?"

Rab glared at the old woman who was snoring by the fire, fighting the urge to shake her awake and demand a cure for his family. But he knew Morven's draught had knocked the witch out until after Halloween, so there was no use even trying. "She's exhausted and sleeping it off, Gil, dinnae mind about her," he told his brother. "Just concentrate on the rest of them—we have to keep them wrapped up so they dinnae catch cold, but keep their brows cool."

Gil nodded grimly, pointing to the buckets of water he'd filled at the pump before the torrential rain started. He was ready for the long night ahead of them. Rab gave him a pat on the shoulder and got to work himself.

As the hours ticked by slowly, and the storm raged closer, the fever seemed to rise with the howling wind. Rab and Gil battled with cold compresses and damp cloths, taking turns to watch their parents and siblings as they muttered and mumbled in their sleep. Rab's brain raced the whole time, trying to come up with another way to get rid of the hag stone before the stroke of midnight.

I need to build a big enough fire, but how am I going to manage it in this downpour? he thought, gazing out into the pitch-black yard. The rain was pounding so hard against the window Rab was half afraid the glass would break. *I cannae build a big fire in here, the kitchen stove wouldnae get near hot enough.*

Suddenly the whole room was lit up in a blaze of light, and Rab jumped back from the window in fright. Seconds later a crack of thunder shook the sky, the foundations of the house trembling in the aftershock.

"Jings!" Gil whistled. "That was close! I hope the barn's safe. Sandy Harris said he'd seen lightning strike so close to a farmhouse that it set a whole barn alight. I wouldnae like to think of that happening here, whit with all our hay and winter grain stored inside. Imagine if it did, Rab! It'd make a blaze bigger than the smithy's forge! Er... whit are you staring at me like that for? Did I say something funny?"

"You're a genius, Gil," Rab grinned. "You just saved the day." He was grabbing his half-dry jacket and a lantern to head outside, when Gil called him back.

"*Now* where are you off to? Ach, dinnae tell me, it's something super-secret and no for the likes of your wee brother," Gil frowned. "You've been acting awfy strange these last few weeks, Rab, and dinnae deny it."

"Look, I'm sorry, Gil. I'll explain everything after, but right now—"

"Dinnae bother." Gil rolled his eyes. "Help me strip these sheets from the wee ones' bed, will you? I need to change the linen."

"Can it no wait? I need to—"

"Can you no see they're drenched in sweat, Rab? You said if we dinnae keep them dry they'll catch a chill."

Rab glanced at the clock. Five minutes to eleven. He still had another hour before midnight. He was sure he could destroy the hag stone by then if he set the hay in the barn ablaze. It would be a disaster losing the whole harvest, but if it saved his family, the loss would be worth it. He could tell his father when he recovered that lightning struck the barn during the storm.

Now he finally had a plan, Rab felt new energy flow through his weary bones. He helped Gil lift Willie and John onto the big bed and set to work stripping the soaked linen from their trundle bed. He was plumping up the straw mattress, when his hand hit an odd lump hidden underneath. He pulled it out and stared at it in shock.

A small poultice bag sat in the palm of his hand, bound tightly with a length of red thread. Even in the flickering candlelight, Rab could see this was exactly the same as the one Morven had tried to give Cousin Betty when she'd injured her arm in the fall.

"Whit the—"

"Whit have you got there? Is it a dead rat?" Gil asked, seeing the shocked look on his brother's face. When he saw what Rab was holding, his own brow furrowed in confusion. "Where did that come from?" he asked. "Doctor Campbell didnae give me anything but this wee medicine bottle that's been about as much use as water from a wishing well."

Rab's mind was reeling, trying to work out what on earth the bag was doing there. "Cousin Betty must've hidden it when I was sleeping the other night," he said slowly. "It's the only explanation."

Gil shook his head. "Nah, she's no got the money for fine cloth like that bag. That kind of weaving can only be bought by the likes of folk at the big house. Have you never seen anything like it afore?"

"Once," Rab had to admit. "Morven had one just like it."

"Oh. Then she must've put it there when she was changing the linen the other day—you know, when we were listening to Cousin Betty's story about the witches at Halloween?"

An awful thought struck Rab, and he strode to the fire, throwing the poultice bag onto the glowing logs. At once the flames shot up, the bag crackling and splitting, the dry herbs inside consumed in an instant. Rab shuddered. In the charred remains at the bottom of the hearth, he was sure he could make out what looked like a small bone, and the tooth of some kind of animal.

"Hey, look!" Gil's shout made him run back to the bed in time to see Willie and John rolling over in their sleep. Their faces had lost the waxy sheen, their cheeks pink once more. Their breathing had eased, and now their sleep was deep and natural, with no more restless twitching.

"Do you think that wee bag was causing the sickness?" Gil gasped.

"I dinnae know, but there's one way to find out. Quick, help me change the sheets and get them back into bed."

When the two small boys were sleeping peacefully in their trundle bed once more, Rab turned his attention to the big bed. With Gil's help, he managed to lift the mattress enough to feel underneath, his heart pounding when he drew out another hidden poultice bag. When it was safely consumed by fire, scattering its contents of crows' feet and cats' claws, Nannie began to recover, the fever leaving her and letting her drift into an easy sleep.

"And Pa?" Gil asked. "Where's his bag?"

They checked down the side of his chair, underneath and inside his pockets, but could find nothing that might make him sick.

"Where would Cousin Betty have put it?" Rab muttered, gazing round the room and trying to remember all the things the old woman had touched.

"I'm telling you, Rab, those wee bags dinnae belong to Cousin Betty," Gil insisted. "You said yourself you'd seen Morven with one just like it."

"Aye, but..." There was somewhere else he'd seen Morven the other night too, somewhere his mother's cousin knew better than to go near. An image formed in his mind, of Morven leafing through the books on his father's desk after supper while Betty washed the dishes in the yard. He remembered the frown on his father's face growing deeper at her disturbing his things until she finally noticed and put them down with an apology.

Rab ran to the parlour, lifting books and paper and rummaging through the desk drawer until he finally found what he was looking for.

There in the drawer behind a bundle of letter paper and sealing wax, was another poultice bag. Rab's hand shook as he carried it to the kitchen fire and dropped it in the flames, his father's fever fading into a deep, natural sleep when its horrible contents were burned.

"Ma's still sick," Gil frowned. "Getting rid of that wee bag under the mattress wasnae enough—there must be another one."

This time Rab knew exactly where to look. He strode over to the bed, lifted the blanket, and pulled something from his mother's pocket.

"Whit have you got there?" Gil asked as Rab headed back to the fire.

Rab held it up without answering. It was a tightly wound spool of thread. When Rab threw it on the fire, the thread burned first, revealing the poultice bag concealed underneath.

He was still staring into the flames when Gil shook him hard by the shoulder. "Right, Rab Burns, I've had enough of your secrecy. I didnae press you afore as I thought you were sweet on that maid Morven, and I didnae want to make you blush with my questions." He dragged Rab over to the table and shoved him onto a stool. "But now you're going to tell me whit all this has been about. And dinnae miss anything out, mind, or I'll know."

Rab took a deep breath and told his brother everything he'd seen since he'd come across the mysterious stone in the field. He told him about the dolls in the kirkyard, the ones he'd seen Betty weave in the yard, and about Betty cursing the factor half to death. Gil's eyes widened when he heard the story of the witches leading Agnes and the baby down the lane, narrowing again when Rab explained everything that Morven had helped him do to get rid of Betty's magic.

By the time Rab had finished his story, Gil was looking at him like he was going to throw a punch. "You, Rab Burns, are the biggest fool who ever walked the face of the earth," he snorted.

"Whit? But—"

"All this time you've been blaming poor Cousin Betty, when it's that pretty wee hussy Morven who's got you wrapped so tight round her pinkie finger you cannae see straight!"

"But she's been helping me!" Rab protested. "She's the one who told me to burn the dolls of Agnes and the baby, and after that the sick animals got better again!"

"Aye, once she removed the poultice bags she hid in the byre and chicken coop, no doubt," Gil scowled. "And whit happened the day after the dolls were burned?"

Rab thought for a bit, then said slowly, "The witches came and tried to lead Agnes and the baby up the lane."

"Exactly! You went and burned the protection charms that Betty made to keep our family safe, that's why!"

"Protection charms?" Rab looked confused. "I've never heard her talk about those afore.

"Course you havenae, you're always up in the loft with your head in a book when Cousin Betty tells us stories round the fire these days. You dinnae know half the folklore she's told us."

Rab thought back to all the times he'd hurried up to the loft after supper for a few snatched moments of peace and quiet with his books.

Between the endless farm work and the non-stop demands for attention from his younger brothers and sisters, he hadn't sat round the fire with Cousin Betty for a long time. Not until he started to suspect she was a witch, and he wanted to keep an eye on her.

Gil hadn't finished giving him a tongue-lashing. He thumped his fist on the table to get Rab's attention again and growled, "And whit happened as soon as you burned all the rest of the dolls Betty made for our family, hmm? Morven was able to put her nasty wee poultice bags under the mattresses and make everyone sick. If Ma hadnae collapsed when she did, Morven would've made it up to the loft to stick one under our mattress too, and we'd be at death's door right now!"

"Aye, but whit about Betty cursing Factor McNab when he shoved her down in the church?" Rab said, trying desperately to come up with an excuse to clear Morven's name. "He got sick that very same day."

"The very day he also shoved *Morven* in the church, you mean?" Gil countered. "The maid who's been living in the big house and can put poultice bags under his mattress any time she chooses?"

"Alright, so it looks bad for her, but it still doesnae explain *this*!" Rab insisted, pulling the hag stone from his pocket and slapping it down on the table. "Every time I've seen witches through it, something bad happens. That's why Morven told me to bind its magic eye with ivy and destroy it in the forge as soon as I got the chance."

Gil slapped his own forehead to stop himself from hitting his big brother and starting a fight. "It's a *hag* stone, Rab! Cousin Betty's told me and the wee ones all about them. It's meant to warn you when witches and bogles are about! That's why Morven had you bind it up and tried to get you to destroy it."

"Oh," Rab said in a small voice, realisation finally dawning. He unwrapped the ivy vines binding the eye carefully, feeling the stone begin to warm again in his hands. "I've been a fool, Gil," he admitted, "but at least no real harm's been done. We managed to stop the sickness. It's just lucky that Agnes and the baby..." he trailed off.

The brothers exchanged horrified looks, then they leapt to their feet, knocking over their stools.

"Morven's taken them!" Gil gasped. "We have to get them back afore the witches gather at midnight!"

"They cannae gather at the old kirk like Morven said," Rab shook his head. "I burned all their summoning dolls, and... oh..." he faltered to a dead stop.

"You mean you burned all of Cousin Betty's protection charms to stop dark magic entering the kirk?" Gil glared at him. "That does it! I dinnae care how tired she is, we need to wake Cousin Betty and get her help."

"That's no going to be possible, Gil," Rab said, his face turning red with shame. "Morven gave me a sleeping draught to dose her with that'll keep her out cold till tomorrow."

"WHIT?" Gil was usually Rab's most easy-going sibling, and his most loyal ally. Now he was clenching his fists in anger, ready to knock his foolish older brother's head off his shoulders.

"We dinnae have time to fight, Gil!" Rab said quickly, pulling on his jacket and boots. "We have to get to the kirkyard to save Agnes and the baby!" He glanced at the clock. It was twenty minutes to twelve. The only way they'd make it on time was to go on horseback.

"Did you remember to put Meg in the byre with the sick horses when the storm broke?" he asked, sighing in relief when his brother shook his head. "Then she'll no be affected by the poultice bag Morven no doubt hid in the byre today to keep the other horses sick. We'll need to saddle her up and take her with us."

"She'll no be in the best of moods being left by herself with only that wee lean-to shed in the field to keep the rain off her. And I cannae see her being up to a gallop in this wild storm," Gil frowned.

"She'll have to be. It's up to you, me and Meg to save Agnes and the baby. We cannae let them down."

Gil swallowed hard, and followed his brother out into the howling gale.

19

Gil was only half right. Meg was in a foul mood at being left outside in the leaky shelter during the storm, but she did her very best to rise to the challenge of galloping down the road in the dark.

She seemed to sense that something was badly wrong, and even with the heavy load of two boys in the saddle, she gave it everything she had without Rab having to urge her on.

Lightning flashed and thunder rolled overhead as they raced down the hill, the wind snatching at Meg's tail and whipping her on faster. The driving rain stung their faces, soaking through their jackets and turning the lanes into swirling rivers. Meg's flying hooves kicked up mud and spray as she dashed through puddles and over broken branches torn from storm-tossed trees. At the bottom of the hill she finally slowed, breathing hard as she headed for the old cottage at Alloway.

"No there, lass," Rab said, patting her neck and tugging the reins to get her to keep going. "We're no stopping just yet."

Meg seemed to realise now where he was taking her, and her trot slowed to an unwilling walk. Rab and Gil jumped down, tugging her reins and leading her on to the line of trees surrounding the old kirk. Despite their words of encouragement, she refused to go any further. Rab gave up, tying her to the old gatepost again, and creeping into the kirkyard with Gil. They ducked down behind one of the few upright headstones, peering at the ruined church in the darkness.

"Are you sure they're gathering here, Rab?" Gil whispered. "I dinnae see anything."

Suddenly there came an enormous clang, so loud it echoed over the howling wind and booming thunder. The church blazed to life, lanterns shaped like skulls grinning from the sill of every window hole. There was another loud clang, and the boys looked up. In the ghostly light, they could see that the tower was no longer empty. An ancient bell had been fixed in place to toll the hour of midnight. The boys shuddered in horror.

"Are we too late, Rab?" Gil asked anxiously.

"I dinnae know. Hush! Something's happening."

A figure dressed in a black cloak came striding from the church, heading for the mausoleum at the back of the kirkyard. When the hood was pulled back, Rab and Gil gasped.

"It's Morven!" Gil said. "Maybe we can talk to her! Maybe—"

"Stay down!" Rab hissed, pulling him back. "It's no only Morven who's out there." He had raised the hag stone to his eye, and through the hole, he could see there were shadowy figures in ragged cloaks circling Morven. They were chanting together, their voices rasping like the caw of hungry crows. "Here—take a look a look for yourself." Rab passed the stone to his brother.

Gil raised it to his eye and peered through. After squinting and turning it this way and that, he handed it back. "I cannae see anything except Morven. There's nothing else there."

But when Rab looked through the eye of the hag stone again, he saw and heard everything.

As the bell continued to toll, the chanting grew louder and louder, the storm rising to a wild shriek. On the final stroke of midnight, the locked gates of the mausoleum split apart, sparks flying in all directions. Red light glowed from inside the burial chamber, and Rab could see flickering tongues of fire licking the walls inside.

Something large and misshapen was moving through the flames. As it stepped into the kirkyard, the veil between the worlds was torn, and thunder rumbled so loud the whole graveyard shook.

"Whit's the matter?" Gil asked when Rab gasped in horror. "Whit's happening?"

"They've gone and summoned something from that old tomb!" Rab whispered, his hands shaking so hard he could barely hold the hag stone steady.

"Whit does it look like?"

"Like a giant shaggy dog with hair as black as pitch. Its face is... Ach, Gil, I cannae describe it, it's too awful for words."

Rab shuddered as he watched the group make their way to the kirk, the shadowy figures bowing and fawning round the enormous creature. Its jaws were so huge that when it growled, Rab could feel the ground shaking beneath his feet. Moonlight flashed off fangs the length of pitchfork prongs, the hideous dog's human hands clenched into fists that hid claws as sharp as daggers. Standing on its hind legs, it was so tall its horned ears brushed the branches of the trees as it passed close to the boys' hiding place.

Rab summoned all of his courage and nudged his brother. "Come on. We have to see whit they're up to, and if Agnes and the baby are in there."

Gil followed him reluctantly, weaving in and out of the fallen headstones until they came to one of the windows. Gil tried to peer over the sill into the church, but Rab pulled him back before he could be spotted.

"Are you daft? They'll catch us for sure if you go sticking your head in!"

"Who'll catch us?" Gil whispered. "I didnae see anyone walking through the kirkyard except Morven."

"I'm telling you, Gil, this whole place is full of

witches," Rab warned. "Keep down—I'll tell you whit I see through the stone."

Very carefully, Rab raised his head high enough to peek over the windowsill and looked through the eye of the hag stone. The old kirk was lit with eerie light, the skull lanterns casting monstrous silhouettes across the walls. Flames from the underworld flickered through the mausoleum's open gateway, bathing the kirkyard in their uncanny red glow.

All of the ivy vines had been torn from the walls and rafters, and now they lay in tangled heaps on the flagstones. In their place, strange symbols had been drawn on the crumbling stone, and on the huge square altar, a man lay bound hand and foot with heavy ropes. He was squirming feebly, and when he turned his ashen face towards the light, Rab recognised him immediately.

"Who is it?" Gil asked breathlessly, interrupting his brother's description.

"It's Factor McNab! He looks awfy sick."

"Whit's he doing there?" Gil frowned.

"I think the witches going to sacrifice him to their master," Rab whispered back. "That's why Morven's been keeping him sick till Halloween and they've brought him here to... Wait. Something's happening!"

He turned his attention to the figures who were gathering in centre of the church, straining his eyes to see what they were waiting for. The giant dog lumbered from the shadows on its hind legs, sitting down on the windowsill opposite Rab and Gil's hiding place. Thrusting a clawed hand into its fur, it drew out a peculiar instrument made of twisted bone pipes and raised it to its lips. Its eyes glowed red as the embers of a fire, and suddenly the whole kirkyard was filled with a hideous wailing sound. The noise shook Rab to the core, and he dropped the stone, ducking down again and trembling in terror.

"Whit is it?" Gil asked, giving him a shake. "Whit did you see?"

"Can you no hear it, Gil?" Rab asked, his voice shaking. Picking up the stone and clutching it in his fist, he could still make out faint strains of the unearthly music. "The witches are dancing to a hornpipe tune—I've never seen anything so terrible!"

"You have to keep looking," Gil urged. "I cannae see for myself."

"I cannae do it, Gil, it's too horrible." Rab shuddered.

"You have to! You still havenae spotted Agnes and Isabella, and we need to find them."

The mention of his sisters was all Rab needed to find the courage to raise the stone to his eye again. He watched as the shadows whirled and reeled, their ragged cloaks swirling around them as they danced to the sinister wails of the hornpipe.

In the very centre of the group, Morven was dancing

the most wildly of all, flinging her cloak to one side, and raising the hem of her skirt as she kicked her heels high in the air. Her cat-like eyes were blazing with triumph, her lips parted to reveal the white fangs that Rab had seen when they'd first met.

It was hard to tear his gaze from the dizzying dance, but Rab knew he had to find his sisters. The light blazing from the leering skull lanterns was starting to hurt his eyes, but he gritted his teeth and stared harder into the hag stone. It grew colder and warmer again as he hunted round the old kirk, leading his gaze to the two figures cloaked in darkness near the doorway. "Can you see them?" he whispered, pointing to where Agnes stood with the baby clutched in her arms.

"Aye, I dinnae need the stone to spy them out," Gil nodded. "Why does Agnes no run away?"

"I think she's asleep. She's under some sort of spell, the way she was that night she wandered from the house up the lane."

"Can we nip in and fetch her out? If they're all that busy with their music and dancing, they might no notice us stealing her away."

"That willnae work." Rab shook his head. "Morven's got one eye on her the whole time. We'll need a distraction if we're to grab her." Rab reached out and snatched up a heavy rock from one of the fallen graves. "Here, take this," he said, thrusting it at his brother. "I'll sneak round to the door, and when I raise my hand, you chuck this right at the big dog. If you knock his hornpipe to the floor, that should get everyone's attention long enough for me to whip Agnes and the baby out the door."

"Whit?" Gil stared at Rab with his mouth hanging open. "That's your plan? How am I meant to chuck a rock at something I cannae even see, you big daftie!"

"You cannae miss it; it's sitting right opposite us. Just lob the rock at the middle of the window hole, and it'll find its mark. Dinnae throw it till I give the signal, mind."

Before Gil could protest any further, Rab crept round the side of the old kirk to the entrance, hiding behind one of the crumbling doorposts and peering inside through the hag stone. What he saw made his heart pound even harder. The shadowy figures were still dancing to the sinister strains of the hornpipe, but Morven had left the group and was marching over to Agnes, a wicked grin on her face. It was too late for Rab to grab his sister now. Morven took Agnes's arm, leading her towards the great dog sitting on the windowsill.

I cannae let that evil beast touch them or they'll be lost to me! Rab thought desperately. He scurried into the kirk, ducking behind the piles of discarded ivy and crawling on his hands and knees towards his sisters. He managed to make it to the final heap of leaves just as Morven reached her master. She gave a low curtsey, then stood to one side.

Whit's she waiting for? Rab wondered, lifting the stone to his eye again. The terrible music sounded loud in his ears once more, and Rab scuttled back when he saw he'd got so close his nose was almost touching the end of the dog's matted tail. It took every ounce of his courage not to turn back and run for his life right there and then.

She's waiting till the music stops! Rab realised. *It's now or never.*

He took a deep breath, and raised his hand, giving the signal to Gil. Something came hurtling through the air, whizzing past Morven's ear and heading straight for the window where the huge dog sat. Before the beast could move, the rock crashed into its pipes, shattering them to pieces.

All at once the music stopped, and the old kirk was plunged into sudden darkness.

20

*F*or an awful moment, Rab thought he'd gone blind. The darkness was so thick and heavy he couldn't even glimpse the moon through the racing storm clouds.

All he could do was reach out and grab the arm he'd seen nearest his hiding place. His hand closed over a slim wrist, and without waiting to find out if he'd got hold of Agnes or Morven, he raced for the dim outline of the doorway at the far end of the kirk.

Tripping over ivy and broken flagstones, he tumbled over the threshold, his heart leaping in relief when he saw he was leading his sleeping sister with the baby, and not the young witch.

His relief was short-lived. As he dashed across the kirkyard, dodging fallen gravestones and tangled bushes, he put the hag stone to his eye to take a quick look behind him.

At once his ears were filled with a loud buzzing, angrier than the roar from an overturned beehive. The wailing of the hornpipe was replaced by the shrieking of witches, who streamed out of the church in pursuit.

The raging wind whipped their ragged hoods back to reveal skeletal heads so shrunken and shrivelled their gaping mouths were just hungry, empty holes. One of the withered skulls still had wisps of white hair sticking out in tufts, and Rab caught a glimpse of a tattered tartan shawl peeking out from under the cloak.

Jessie McGuire! Rab gasped. *She's the one who killed Morven's family and turned Morven into a witch!*

Lightning flashed from the storm clouds above, and Rab yelped in fright when he saw who was leading the charge. Morven had leapt onto the back of the great black dog and was clinging on to its shaggy hair. Its claws tore at the earth as it crashed over the gravestones towards them, urged on by its furious rider.

"Gil!" Rab yelled, grabbing Agnes round the waist and half-carrying her the rest of the way. "Gil! Where are you?"

"Here! Come on, I'll pull Aggie up!"

Gil had already untied Meg from the gatepost and was sitting in the saddle, reaching down for his sisters. When he had one arm safely round Agnes and the baby, and the other hand grasping the reins, he gave Meg a sharp kick, and Rab barely had time to leap on behind him as the old horse took off down the lane.

"Where are you going, you daftie?" Rab protested. "We need to get back to the farm!"

"There's no time!" Gil couldn't see the witches or

hear their howling, but he could see Morven charging towards them on a great black shadow, and that was terrifying enough. "Do you no remember Betty's story?" he shouted above the roar of the storm. "We need to get to the Brig o' Doon! The witches cannae cross running water. We'll be safe on the other side."

"We'll never make it!" Rab yelled.

"We have to!" Gil shouted back, his face set in grim determination as he urged Meg on faster. Rab was too scared to argue. Turning back, he clung on with one hand and raised the hag stone to his eye with the other.

Morven and the monstrous dog were almost upon them, the ghostly figures of witches gliding over the ground behind them at breakneck speed. Morven was gnashing her teeth in rage, her hair loose and writhing in the wind like a nest of snakes. The great dog's eyes burned red in the darkness like giant storm lanterns warning of danger. All around them the lightning flashed, the thunder splitting the air and shaking the ground beneath Meg's galloping hooves.

"Are they close?" Gil yelled, too busy clinging on to Agnes and the baby and steering Meg with his free hand to look back.

"We're nearly there, Gil, keep going!" Rab urged, slapping Meg's rump to get her to move faster. The old horse panted and snorted, straining every muscle as she charged on, her eyes wide with terror.

Through the driving rain, they could see the curve of the river behind a screen of trees. The old bridge was up ahead, the swollen water rushing beneath its broad arch.

"There it is, Gil! Just a wee bit more and—Eek!" Rab yelped. A hand brushed his back, reaching for him in the dark. When the next flash of lightning lit up the sky, Rab could see Morven leaning forward over the great dog's neck, stretching out to try to grab him. Her hand was now a gnarled and withered claw, her nails lengthening to talons that scraped Meg's flanks.

Meg whinnied and galloped harder, the rain washing the froth from her mouth as she gasped for breath.

"Come on, Gil!" Rab shouted as Morven lunged again, her fangs snapping and her eyes filled with hate. Just as they reached the bridge and Meg's hooves clattered over the cobble stones, her hand caught the end of Meg's tail, tugging hard. The old horse reared up, nearly throwing the children to the ground. The dog's jaws opened wide, ready to swallow them whole. Gil clung tight to Agnes and the baby, fighting for control as Meg reared and plunged.

"Now, Meg!" Rab cried, giving her rump a final slap. Meg threw her weight forward, reaching the centre of the bridge despite Morven still clinging tightly to her tail.

The dog launched itself at them, its jaws gaping hungrily. As the great beast crossed the keystone of the bridge, another flash of lightning split the sky directly above the old kirk. The lightning crackled to earth, and a huge explosion rocked the kirkyard, pieces of stone flying so high into the air that Rab could see them rise above the treetops. Sparks flew from the monstrous dog's mouth and it stumbled back, dragging Morven with it. There was a terrible hissing noise in the dark, and suddenly the dog burst into flames. Morven disappeared in the inferno, fire shooting down her withered hand and setting Meg's tail alight. The old horse gave a last whinny of fear and cantered across the bridge, leaping onto the path on the far side.

"Did we do it?" Gil gasped. "Are we safe?"

Rab looked back through the hag stone. The storm had died to a soft whisper, and now all he could see on the bridge was a huge pile of ash that smoked and sizzled in the rain. "Aye, Gil," he said, half dazed. "It's over.

"Can we go home now, d'you think?"

Rab hesitated. He was almost certain the witches had been destroyed in the fire, but he wanted to make absolutely sure before they crossed the bridge again.

"Best wait till sunrise. Meg's that tired she can hardly stay upright, and I cannae blame her. Look whit's happened to her tail!" He held up the burnt stump, blowing on it to extinguish the last of the embers. "Head to Doonside Castle, it's just up ahead. We'll rest Meg there for the night and go back at dawn."

Meg trudged wearily down the road, turning off when they came to the ruins of the three-storey tower that had once been a fine castle. The rain had eased to a fine drizzle, but they were soaked through and glad of the shelter. When Rab and Gil helped Agnes down from the saddle, they were worried to see she was still unresponsive. Her eyes were open, but she seemed to be in a deep sleep.

"Whit do you think's wrong with her?" Gil asked, taking the baby and leading Agnes into the tower basement that still had its vaulted roof intact.

"I dinnae know. Last time she woke up when the witches disappeared. Maybe Morven drugged her with something," Rab frowned, finding an old post to tie Meg's reins to and hunting round for some dry firewood. Day labourers had been using the tower as a waypoint on their travels to find work, and there was a pile of logs and kindling in the corner. Rab got a fire going with the tinderbox in his pocket, and soon their clothes were steaming as they dried in the heat.

"How's Isabella?" Rab asked, watching Gil gently rock the baby back and forth.

"She's the same as Agnes. She awake, but no responding. Rab, d'you think we've lost them? Now that Morven's gone, d'you think they'll stay like this?"

"No if I can help it," Rab growled. He reached over and shook Agnes by the shoulders. His sister wobbled, righted herself, then continued staring into the fire without even looking at him.

"It's no use, I cannae—"

"Hey! Whit's that?" Gil pointed to a small square of cloth that had fallen from their sister's pocket when Rab shook her. Rab picked it up, turning it over and examining it in the firelight.

"It's that wee handkerchief that Morven gave her— you know, when she fell in the market and cut her knee. She sewed Aggie's initials into it when she was over one night." The embroidered letters *A.B.* gleamed in the firelight, and Rab took a closer look at them. "Whit the..? Gil! These have no been sewn with thread."

"Whit then?" Gil asked.

"It's Aggie's hair! I remember her pulling some out when we went down to see Cousin Betty. She pretended it was an accident." Rab reached over and checked the baby's blanket. There, in the corner, were the initials *I.B.*, sewn in the same colour as Isabella's downy hair. "That wicked wee minx! She must've done that when Agnes took the baby to Doonholm."

"You mean those wee scraps of cloth are magic spells?" Gil gasped.

"They might well be. There's only one way to find out." Rab ripped the corner of the blanket away, tearing off the initials. He threw it on the fire along with the handkerchief, watching them turn to ash. Suddenly

Isabella began to stir in Gil's arms, squirming about and breaking into a hungry wail.

Agnes sat up straighter, rubbing her eyes and yawning loudly.

"Whit's going on?" she blinked. "Have I been sleepwalking again?"

"Aye, that's right." Rab winked at Gil, warning him to hold his tongue. "You walked that far with the baby, me and Gil had to come looking for you on Meg."

"But whit about the fever?" Agnes gasped. "Are Ma and Pa and—"

"They're all better now. Doctor Campbell set them to rights with his medicine," Gil told her, rocking Isabella until she settled down again.

Agnes let out a long sigh of relief, but her eyes were still worried as she glanced at Rab. "D'you think Ma and Pa will give me a month's worth of punishments for this?" she asked him.

"Only if they find out," Rab smiled. "And I'm no going to tell them. Are you Gil?"

"Tell them whit?" Gil raised an eyebrow. "As long as we sneak in afore everyone's up, then as far as they know, we've been asleep in our beds all night."

Agnes's shoulders slumped in relief. She looked exhausted. Rab put his arm round her, and she rested her head on his shoulder. "Talking of sleep, you could do with some, Aggie. Have a wee rest, and me and Gil will have you and the baby home afore you know it."

"Thanks, Rab. You're the best big brother a lassie could wish for," Agnes mumbled sleepily as she snuggled into his neck.

I'm certainly no that, Rab thought to himself. *But I'm going to try harder from now on. I've been so busy complaining about how hard things are at the farm I didnae realise how lucky I was to have such a family as mine. From now on, I willnae be taking them for granted. Especially no Cousin Betty,* he added, clutching the hag stone in his pocket tightly and watching the fire crackle as they waited for dawn.

21

It was another few days before Rab got a chance to go down to the old cottage at Alloway to visit Cousin Betty.

The wild storm had caused a lot of damage to the farm buildings, and with their father needing time to recover his full strength after the fever, it fell to Rab and Gil to do most of the work. Rab was too relieved to see his parents getting better and his younger siblings getting up to mischief again to complain, though.

At dinner one afternoon, there came a knock on the door. When William Burns got up to open it, Agnes made a snatch for a bit of Rab's scone. For once, he didn't smack her hand, giving her a sideways glance and grinning at her instead. Agnes smiled back, popping the crumbs in her mouth and giving him a playful nudge under the table.

"You're getting slow in your old age, Rab."

"I'm just feeding you up so you'll grow big and strong and take over my field work. Then I can sit by the fire all day and you can plough the fields," he shot back.

"If Pa would only let me near the plough horses, I bet

I'd get the furrows cut faster and straighter than you any day!"

"Whit do you bet?"

"All your scones and bannock from now till next Halloween."

"Och, that's too rich a bet for me," Rab laughed. "Here, take this one, and dinnae challenge me to competitions I'll never win." He handed his scone over, and Agnes beamed at him in delight.

They'd been getting on much better since they crept back into the house early in the morning after Halloween, settling Isabella back in her crib and sneaking off to bed before their parents woke up. Cousin Betty had given them all an odd look when she'd risen from her chair and rubbed the sleep from her eyes. She hadn't questioned them, though. She just slipped off home after checking that the family had all recovered from their fevers. Rab was desperate to get an opportunity to talk to her about everything that had happened, but she hadn't visited them since that day.

More than anything, he wanted the chance to apologise for his behaviour.

"Is everything all right, William?" Mrs Burns asked, seeing her husband close the door with a frown after exchanging a few brief words with a delivery boy.

"Aye, but..." William Burns stared in disbelief at the letter he'd been handed, shaking a few coins from the envelope onto the table. "Factor McNab's written to say we overpaid our October rent. He says the chickens Rab delivered the other week were enough."

"Whit?" His wife gazed at the coins as though they'd rolled down from the end of a rainbow. "Why would a man like that return a payment, when he's been turning the thumbscrews on us ever since he took the job?"

William shook his head. "I cannae fathom the man. Maybe his brush with death and sudden recovery has taught him a wee bit of Christian kindness."

Rab and Gil exchanged glances. Only they knew what really happened at Halloween. With Agnes sleeping soundly on Meg, they'd visited the old kirk on the way back home in the early light, untying the spell-bound factor from his stone altar and leading him back up the lane. They'd left him fast asleep at the gates to Doonholm, burning the enchanted handkerchief they found in his pocket as soon as they got home. With the witches and their curses gone, he'd made a full recovery. His good mood at getting out of his sick bed wouldn't last, though, and Rab was sure it wouldn't be long before the factor was back to his mean, penny-pinching ways.

Just as well he was asleep like Agnes the whole time, Rab thought. *The truth's best kept between me and Gil. But I cannae wait to tell the whole story to Cousin Betty.*

As though reading his mind, his mother said, "Rab, if you're done eating, will you nip down to Alloway for me?

I'd like you to take some scones down to thank Cousin Betty for all her hard work when we werenae well."

"Can I come?" Nannie asked. "I want to see Cousin Betty!"

"Me too!" Wee Willie piped up.

"And me!" John said, not entirely sure what he was volunteering for, but not wanting to be left out whatever it was.

"I thought you three could come up the brae with me and Agnes this afternoon and gather the chestnuts the wind's blown down," Gil said, giving his brother the excuse he needed to see Betty alone. "There'll be a fine late crop this year, and we can roast them over the fire tonight. Whit do you say?"

"Aye! Let's go!" the children chorused, grabbing their shoes and jackets.

"Thanks, Gil," Rab whispered, "I owe you one."

"Only one?" Gil winked at his brother. "If I keep the wee ones busy for you, then just make sure you tell me everything Cousin Betty has to say. I dinnae want to get left out this time. Deal?"

"Deal." Rab smiled and held out his hand for his brother to shake, yelping when Gil slapped a piece of soggy turnip from the stew pot into his palm instead.

"Ach, Gil! You manky wee bogle. I'll drown you in the duck pond for that!"

"Maybe, but you'll have to catch me first, and we

both know you're too slow!" Gil laughed, hustling the children out of the door before Rab could chase him.

Rab laughed too, taking his mother's basket and heading to the near field to see if Meg was up to a short walk.

He was half expecting the old horse to be in a huff with him after everything she'd been through at Halloween. But Meg was too loyal to hold a grudge, and she came trotting over to nuzzle him, trying to pinch the scones from his mother's basket while he saddled her up.

"Hey! You're as bad as Agnes! At this rate I'll have nothing but crumbs to give to Cousin Betty as a peace offering."

He trotted down the lane, waving to his brothers and sisters who were climbing up the hills to the small copse of horse chestnut trees. Meg was still a bit stiff from her wild gallop, and her stump of a tail bounced heavily behind her as a reminder of what she'd been through, but she walked down to Alloway happily enough, her head held high as though she was proud of what she'd done for him.

When they reached the cottage, Betty wasn't at home.

Where can she have got to? Rab wondered. *It's no like her to... Oh.*

It suddenly dawned on him where she would be. The Halloween storm had kept the rain pouring down for three whole days, and it was the first clear, dry day they'd had since then. Rab led Meg down the lane, heading for the graveyard and the old kirk that lay beyond the line of trees. He expected Meg to put up her usual fight when they reached the outskirts of the kirkyard, but she surprised him by walking past the gateposts and stepping straight into the cemetery without the slightest protest. She headed for the yew tree, rubbing her itching flanks against its rough bark and cropping the grass hungrily.

Rab stared at her in amazement. But then he realised it wasn't Meg that had changed, it was the kirkyard itself. The whole atmosphere was different. The autumn sun was shining down through the treetops, glistening on the leaves and shimmering on the small puddles that had gathered in hollowed-out stones. The air was no longer cold, and the sense of foreboding Rab had felt before was gone.

That wasn't the only change. The lightning that struck when the great dog had crossed the keystone of the Doon bridge hadn't hit the kirk itself, but the mausoleum standing at the back of the kirkyard. The whole burial chamber had crumbled to dust, and all that was left of the monument was a pile of broken stones and twisted metal.

"Are you going to stand there gawping all day, Rab, or are you going to give me a hand?" a familiar voice asked.

Rab turned to see Cousin Betty hobbling from the church, carrying what looked like a pile of shattered bones.

"Right, that's the last of them," she said, dumping them into the deep hole she'd dug at the base of the yew tree. "Make yourself useful and fill it in for me, would you? My old back's no up to the job this time."

"This time?" Rab asked, taking the spade and shovelling earth over the remains of the sinister hornpipe and skull lanterns.

"Aye, *this* time," Betty repeated, throwing him a wink. "Who d'you think it was who cleared up the mess when that daftie Tam went and disturbed the witches' revels here fifty years ago? That's when I first learned about their wicked ways, and I've been warding against them ever since."

"You could've told me, Cousin Betty," Rab sighed. "I might no have made such a fool of myself over that witch Morven, and let her trick me into thinking it was you who was responsible for all this."

"Is that whit she told you?" Betty frowned, her wrinkles growing so deep her cloudy eyes were almost lost in them. "I wondered why you'd been acting so strange."

"I'm sorry, Cousin Betty," Rab said, too shamefaced to lift his eyes from the ground where he was shovelling soil. "I was wrong to trust Morven and treat you the way I did. And as for giving you that tea with her potion in it, I... I..."

"Ach, it's my own fault," Betty said, patting him on

the shoulder. "You're a smart lad, Rab, and I should've trusted you with the truth. I'll no make that mistake again. It's no your fault you were fooled by her pretty face and couldnae see the evil heart she had underneath."

"I do feel a wee bit sorry for her, though," Rab sighed, leaning on the spade. "Jessie McGuire must've enchanted her and killed her family, turning her into a witch, like Morven was trying to do to Agnes."

"Just be grateful she didnae manage it," Betty told him. "You were lucky to have the help that you did."

"Aye, Gil made me see sense in the nick of time," Rab nodded.

"I didnae mean that daft wee gowk, I meant the stone you've got in your pocket."

Rab blinked at her in surprise, pulling the hag stone out and holding it up. "How did you know I had it?"

"Because it left me a few weeks ago, and I knew it had gone to find someone younger to stop the witches this time."

"You mean this was yours?" Rab gasped.

"Aye. It found me fifty years ago—that's how I helped Tam escape the witches back then. But *that's* no the version of the story I'll be telling your family round the hearth!"

"Then it's yours, Cousin Betty. Here, take it back."

The old woman shook her head, closing his hand over the stone. "You're its keeper now, Rab. It needs someone younger, and it'll always find its way back to you. Here."

She pulled a length of cord from her pocket, passing it through the eye of the hag stone and hanging it around Rab's neck. "That's better, it'll no slip out of your pocket now. Tuck it under your shirt, mind. You dinnae want your parents asking any questions about it."

"Do you think I'll have to deal with witches again, then?" Rab asked, hiding the stone under his shirt. Its polished surface felt smooth against his skin, but it had lost its cold edge, nestling snugly against his chest as though it belonged there.

"Maybe, lad, maybe. Old Nick will no be using that gateway any longer." Betty pointed to the ruins of the mausoleum. "But there's plenty more creatures out there in the dark and shadows. Keep your eyes open, lad. Now the stone's found you, it'll make sure you do your bit to keep the evil at bay."

Rab gulped. "You think I'm ready for such a big job, Cousin Betty?"

The old woman gave him a toothless smile. "None of us are ever ready, Rab. Being willing is whit counts. Now, get back home afore your ma sends out a search party. And dinnae forget to thank her for sending me a basket full of her best crumbs."

"Eh? Ach, Meg! You greedy old nag!"

Meg looked up, chewing on the last of the scones Rab had left in the basket on the grass. He couldn't be sure, but in the glowing sunlight, it looked like Meg was grinning.

"Well, I cannae begrudge you that wee treat after everything you've done for us," he muttered, getting into the saddle and giving Cousin Betty a last wave as they walked up the lane.

The loyal old horse gave a loud snort, and Rab had a funny feeling she knew he was thanking her.

As they made their way slowly up the road to Mount Oliphant, the late afternoon sun turned the hills and fields to spun gold, lighting up the sky and glittering on the sea in the distance. Rab smiled as he caught sight of the farm on the hillside, its familiar outline a welcome sight after such a hair-raising adventure.

"Come on, Meg," he said, urging her into a trot. "We're nearly home."

Home.

It was the first time he'd ever called it that and meant it. Whatever strange magic and monsters were out there, lurking in the mists and shadows, he felt ready for them.

He might wish for more education, more time for friends and more meat at the supper table, but he had his family, and he had his home at Mount Oliphant, and no matter what might happen in the future, today he was thankful just to be Rab Burns, the boy farmer.

THE END

GLOSSARY

Aboot—about

Afore—before

Aye—yes

Bairns—children

Bannock—a type of flat bread cooked on a griddle

Bellows—a device for a blacksmith to blow air into a fire to make it hotter

Biggin—a house or cottage

Birkie—a conceited man

Blether—talk idly

Bletherskate—someone who talks at great length

Bogle—an ugly or terrifying supernatural being

Brae—a steep bank or hillside

Brambles—blackberries

Cannae—can't

Crabbit—grumpy

Didnae—didn't

Dinnae—don't

Doesnae—doesn't

Doddle—easy task

Factor—a property manager who oversees the running of an estate on behalf of the owner and collects rent from tenants

Gadding—going from place to place in search of pleasure

Gowk—an awkward or foolish person

Griddle—a heavy, flat iron plate used for cooking

Hadnae—hadn't

Hasnae—hasn't

Havenae—haven't

Isnae—isn't

Jings—used to express surprise

Kirk—church

Lassie—girl

Manky—dirty and unpleasant

Mausoleum—a building housing a burial chamber or tomb

Midden—a dunghill or rubbish heap

No—not

Old Nick—used as a name for the devil

Scullery—a small room at the back of the kitchen used for washing dishes and other dirty work

Sheugh—ditch

Smithy—blacksmith, or the forge where they work

Tatties—potatoes

Tawse—a leather strap used for punishing school children

Wasnae—wasn't

Wee—little

Wheesht!—silence!

Whit—what

Willnae—won't

ACKNOWLEDGEMENTS

The support of family and friends plays an important part in the development of an author's career, and I want to thank all of the people who have given me the encouragement I needed to get to the publication stage with my work (you know who you are!).

In particular, my mother and my brother Martin have been instrumental in my evolution from aspiring writer to fully-fledged author, and I am incredibly grateful for their unwavering support.

Huge thanks to Anne Glennie, Cranachan's guiding light, who dedicates her time and energy wholeheartedly to each book she works on, and whose effort and commitment has been a real source of inspiration.

Thanks also to the authors of Clan Cranachan, whose enthusiastic cheerleading of each other's work has created a supportive environment which is a joy to be part of.

Elise Carmichael, the illustrator of this book, deserves a special mention and warm thanks for all of her hard work. She went the extra mile during the cover design stages, and I couldn't be happier with the amazing result.

Finally, I'd like to thank the Robert Burns World Federation for all of the work they do promoting the poetry of Robert Burns in schools and encouraging new readers to discover the magic in his writing. I have happy memories of entering the Burns competitions they ran when I was in primary school (I still have the certificates!), and it was my study of Tam o' Shanter all those years ago which planted the first seeds of this novel.

In order to support their work inspiring the next generation of Scottish writers, *20% of the author royalties for this novel will be donated to the Robert Burns World Federation.*

ABOUT THE AUTHOR

A lifelong storyteller and daydreamer, Victoria Williamson is a children's author and teacher who has lived and worked in Africa, China, America and the UK.

Victoria grew up in Kirkintilloch, north Glasgow, surrounded by hills on the edge of a forest estate where many of her early ghost stories and fantasy tales were born amid the magical trees and spooky old ruined buildings.

After studying Physics at the University of Glasgow, she set out on her own real life adventures, which included teaching maths and science in Cameroon, training teachers in Malawi, teaching English in China and working with children with special needs in the UK.

Her previous novels, *The Fox Girl and the White Gazelle* (2018 – Floris Books), and *The Boy with the Butterfly Mind* (2019 – Floris Books) were based on her experiences of teaching children with diverse backgrounds and have been shortlisted for a number of awards.

Victoria divides her time between writing, visiting schools and speaking at festivals to encourage children of all ages to write their own stories and exercise their imaginations.

strangelymagical.com

@strangelymagic